"It was just a kiss."

Flynn raked a hand through his dark hair as he continued, "Between two consenting adults, I might add. Now, if we'd ended up in bed I might be able to understand you feeling slightly... maneuvered."

"I barely know you," Marigold snapped.

Dark eyebrows rose mockingly. "Flynn Moreau, single and of sound mind," he offered lazily. "Anything else you'd deem important?"

"Plenty."

"Then we'll have to see to that," he said very softly.

He was *interested* in her? A man like him—successful, wealthy, charismatic and powerful? She couldn't quite believe it....

HELEN BROOKS lives in Nothamptonshire, England, and is married with three children. As she is a committed Christian, busy housewife and mother, her spare time is at a premium, but her interests include reading, swimming, gardening and walking her two energetic, inquisitive and very endearing young dogs. Her long-cherished aspiration to write became a reality when she put pen to paper on reaching the age of forty, and sent the result off to Mills and Boon.

Look out for Helen Brooks's next book, written especially for the Harlequin Presents® 9 to 5 mini-series. *Sleeping Partners* is on sale early next year.

Don't miss any of our special offers. Write to us at the following address for information on our newest releases.

Harlequin Reader Service
U.S.: 3010 Walden Ave., P.O. Box 1325, Buffalo, NY 14269
Canadian: P.O. Box 609, Fort Erie, Ont. L2A 5X3

Helen Brooks
CHRISTMAS AT HIS COMMAND

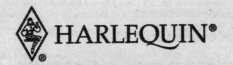

HARLEQUIN®

TORONTO • NEW YORK • LONDON
AMSTERDAM • PARIS • SYDNEY • HAMBURG
STOCKHOLM • ATHENS • TOKYO • MILAN • MADRID
PRAGUE • WARSAW • BUDAPEST • AUCKLAND

ISBN 0-373-12292-6

CHRISTMAS AT HIS COMMAND

First North American Publication 2002.

Copyright © 2002 by Helen Brooks.

CHAPTER ONE

'OH, NO, please, *please* don't do this to me.' Marigold shut her eyes, thick dark lashes falling briefly on honey-smooth skin before she raised them again to glare at the dashboard in front of her. 'What are you doing to me, Myrtle? We're miles from anywhere and the weather's foul. You can't have a tantrum now. I didn't mean it a mile or two back when I called you crabby.'

The ancient little car didn't reply by so much as a cough or a splutter, but Marigold suspected there was a distinctly smug air of 'You should think before you speak' to Myrtle's demeanour as the car's four wheels settled themselves more comfortably into the two inches of snow coating the road in front of them. The old engine had been hiccuping for the last half an hour or so before dying completely.

Great. Just great. Marigold peered out into the driving snow that was already coating the windscreen now the wipers had ceased their labouring. In another hour it would be dark, and here she was, stuck in the middle of nowhere and with what looked like a very cold walk in front of her. She couldn't stay in the car—she'd freeze to death out here if no one came along—and for the last little while there hadn't been sight of a house or any dwelling place on the road.

She reached out and unhooked the piece of paper with the directions to Sugar Cottage off the dashboard, wondering if she had taken a wrong turning somewhere. But she hadn't, she assured herself in the next moment. She knew she hadn't. And Emma had warned her the cottage was remote, but that had been exactly what she wanted. It still was, if only she could get to the flipping place!

She studied the directions again, frowning slightly as she concentrated on working out how far she still had to go along the country track, her fine curved brows drawing together over eyes which were of a vivid violet-blue. The last building had been that 'olde-worlde' thatched pub she'd passed about ten miles back, and then she'd driven on for—she consulted the directions again—probably another mile or two before turning off the main road into a country lane. And then it had been just a rough track for the last few miles. Perhaps it wasn't so far now to Sugar Cottage? Whatever, she had no choice but to start walking.

She allowed herself one last heartfelt sigh before turning and surveying the laden back seat. Right. Her wellington boots were in her old university knapsack along with an all-enveloping cagoule that nearly came down to her toes! She had packed her torch in there too after Emma had emphasised umpteen times how isolated and off the beaten track the cottage was. Mind you, Emma had been more concerned about the electricity failing— a common occurrence in winter apparently—or Marigold having to dig her way to the car from the front door. They'd both assumed she'd actually *reach* the cottage before any dramas reared their heads.

There was a large manor house across the other side of the valley, Emma had said, but basically the small cottage in Shropshire she had inherited from her grandmother in the spring was secluded enough for one to feel insulated from the outside world.

And right now, Marigold told herself firmly as she struggled into her thick, warm fleece before pulling on the cagoule, that was worth braving a snowstorm for. No telephone and no TV, Emma had continued when she'd offered Marigold the use of the cottage over Christmas— her grandmother had refused to allow any such suspect modern inventions over the threshold! And the old lady had baked all her own bread, kept chickens and a cow in the paddock next to the house, and after her husband died had remained by herself in her home until passing away peacefully in her sleep aged ninety-two. Marigold thought she'd have liked to meet Emma's grandmother.

The cagoule and wellington boots on, Marigold quickly repacked the knapsack with a few necessary provisions from the bags of groceries piled high on the front passenger seat. She would have to leave her suitcase and everything else for now, she decided regretfully. If she could just reach the cottage tonight she'd sort everything out tomorrow somehow. Of course, it would have helped if she hadn't left her mobile phone in the flat back in London, but she'd been three-quarters of the way here when she'd remembered it was still sitting by her bed at home and it had been far too late then to go back for it.

The last thing she did before leaving the warm sanctuary of Myrtle's metal bosom was to stuff the directions to Sugar Cottage in her cagoule pocket. Then she climbed out of the car, locked the door and squared her shoulders.

Finding the cottage in a snowstorm was nothing, not after what she'd been through in the last few months, she told herself stoutly. And if nothing else it would be a different sort of Christmas, certainly different to the one she'd had planned with Dean. No doubt right now he and Tamara were sunning themselves on the Caribbean beach *she'd* chosen out of the glossy travel brochures they'd pored over for hours when they'd still been together. She couldn't believe he was actually taking Tamara on the holiday which was to have been their honeymoon. On top of all the lies and deceit, that had been the ultimate betrayal, and when one of their mutual friends—awkward and embarrassed—had tipped her the wink about it she'd felt like going straight round to Dean's flat and socking him on the jaw.

She hadn't, of course. No, she had maintained the aloof, dignified silence she'd adopted since that first white-hot outburst when she'd found out about the other woman and told Dean what a low-down, slimy, no-good creep he was as she'd thrown her engagement ring in his blustering face.

The familiar welling of tears made itself felt deep in her chest and she gritted her teeth resolutely. No more crying. No more wailing after what was dead and finished. She had made herself that promise a couple of weeks ago and she'd die before she went back on it. She wanted nothing to do with the opposite sex for the foreseeable future, and if this cottage was really as far away in the backwoods as Emma had suggested she might just make her an offer for it now. Emma had confided she was thinking of putting it on the market in the new year.

Marigold began walking, hardly aware of the snowflakes swimming about her as her thoughts sped on. She'd been thinking for some time, ever since the split with Dean at the end of the summer, in fact, that she needed a complete change of direction and lifestyle.

She had been born and bred in London, gone to university there, where she'd started dating Dean in the last year of her art and design degree, and after her course ended had found a well-paid job in a small firm specialising in graphic design. She had worked mainly on posters and similar projects to start with, but when the firm had decided to diversify into all manner of greetings cards her extensive portfolio of work—accumulated throughout her training years—had come into its own, and she had found herself in the happy position of working solely on the new venture. Dean had proposed about the same time—twelve months ago now—and she had thought her future was all set. Until Tamara Jaimeson came on the scene.

'Ow!' As though the thought of the other girl had conjured up an evil genie, Marigold suddenly found herself falling full length as her foot caught in what was obviously a pothole in the rough road. The snow cushioned her landing to a certain extent but when she tried to stand again she found she'd wrenched her ankle enough to make her grimace with pain, and now all thoughts of a remote little studio, somewhere where she could freelance both to her present firm—who had already expressed interest in such a proposition—and others, couldn't have been further from Marigold's mind.

She could only have been limping along for ten minutes before she heard the magical sound of a car's engine behind her, but it had seemed like ten hours, such was the pain in her foot.

It was still quite light but she dug into her knapsack and brought out the torch nevertheless, moving to the edge of the road by the snow-covered hedgerow. She couldn't risk the driver of the approaching vehicle missing her in the atrocious weather conditions.

The massive 4x4 was cutting through the snow with an imperious regality which highlighted its noble birth and also underlined poor Myrtle's less exalted beginnings, but the driver had already seen her and was slowing down, even before she switched on the torch and waved it frantically.

'Oh, thank you, thank you.' She almost went headlong again as she stumbled over to the open window on the driver's side. 'My car's broken down and I don't know how far I've got to go, and I fell over and I've twisted my ankle—'

'OK, slow down, slow down.'

It wasn't so much the cold, impatient tone of his voice which stopped Marigold in full flow, but her first sight of the big dark man sitting behind the steering wheel. He was handsome in a rather tough, rugged way, but it was the cool grey eyes which could have been formed in a block of hard granite that caused her to be momentarily lost for words.

'I take it that's your car back there, which means you could only be making for Sugar Cottage.'

'Does it?' Marigold stared at him stupidly. 'Why?'

'Because it's the only other house in the valley apart from mine,' he replied—obviously, Marigold's mind emphasised a second too late.

'So you must be Emma Jones; Maggie's granddaughter,' the chilly voice continued flatly.

'I—'

'I understand you came once before to look over the cottage when I was abroad. I was sorry to have missed you then.'

The words themselves could have been friendly, however, the tone in which they were spoken made them anything but, and Marigold blinked at the quiet enmity coming her way.

'I promised myself after that occasion that if I ever had the chance to give you a piece of my mind, I would,' he said with soft venom.

'Look, Mr…?'

'Moreau,' he provided icily.

'Look, Mr Moreau, I think I ought to explain—'

'Explain?'

Marigold had heard of incidents where one person could freeze another into silence and she hadn't actually experienced it until now, but in the last moment or two he had shifted slightly in his seat and now the grey eyes had taken on a silver hue which turned them into two flares of cold white light.

'Explain what?' he continued curtly. 'The reason why not one of your family, you included, saw fit to visit an old lady in the last twelve months before her death? The odd letter or two, the occasional phone call to the village shop that delivered her groceries every week was supposed to suffice, was it? Messages delivered secondhand can't compare to flesh and blood reality, Miss Jones. Oh, I know she could be difficult, recalcitrant and obstinate to a point where you could cheerfully have strangled her, but didn't any of you understand the fierce plea for independence and the pride behind it? She was an old lady, for crying out loud. Ninety-two years old! Didn't *any* of you have the imagination and the sensitivity to realise that behind her awkwardness and perversity she was crying out to be told she was still loved and wanted for the woman she was?'

'Mr Moreau—'

'But it was simpler and easier to write her off as bigoted and impossible,' he bit out savagely. 'That way you could all get on with your nice, orderly lives with your consciences clean and unsmirched.'

Anger was beginning to surface inside Marigold, not least because of this man's arrogant refusal to allow her to get a word in edgeways. He had clearly been seething about what he saw as the neglect of Emma's family towards the old lady for a long time, but he wasn't giving her a chance to explain who she was or what she was doing here!

'You don't understand. I'm not—'

'Responsible?' Again he cut her off, his eyes like polished crystal. 'That's too easy a get-out clause, Miss Jones. It might suit you to give out the air of helpless femininity in the present situation in which you find yourself, but it doesn't fool me. Not for a second! And while you are considering how much you can make on selling your grandmother's home—a home she fought tooth and nail to keep going, I might add—you could consider the blood, sweat and tears that went into her remaining here all her life. And there were tears, don't fool yourself about that. And caused by you and the rest of your miserable family.'

'You have absolutely no right to talk to me like this.' Marigold was at the point of hitting him.

'No?' His voice was softer now but curiously more deep and disturbing than its previous harsh tone. 'So you aren't looking to sell the old lady's pride and joy, then? The home she fought so hard to keep?'

Marigold opened her mouth to fire back a rejoinder but then, in the next instant, it dawned on her that that was exactly what Emma was planning to do and for a moment the realisation floored her.

'I thought so.' She was at the receiving end of that deadly stare again. 'How someone like you can have the same blood as that courageous old lady flowing through their veins beats me, I tell you straight. You and the rest of your family aren't worthy to lick her boots.'

Marigold stared at him through the snowflakes that had settled on her eyelashes. She was about to tell him she *didn't* have the same blood, that she was in fact no relation at all to Emma's grandmother, when the hot rage which was bubbling checked her words. Let him think what he liked, the arrogant swine! She would rather struggle on all night than ask him for help or explain he'd got it all wrong. The man was a bully, whatever the facts behind all he had said. He knew she'd had to abandon her car and that she had hurt herself, yet he'd still been determined to browbeat her and have his say. Well, he could take a running jump! She wasn't going to explain a thing and he could drive off in his nice warm car, knowing that he had had his pound of flesh. The rotten, stinking—

'Lost for words, Miss Jones?' he enquired softly, the tone of his voice making the icy air around Marigold strike warm.

'Not at all.' She drew herself up to her full five feet four inches and never had she wished so hard she was half a foot or so taller. 'I was just wondering whether it was worth wasting any breath on such an unsavoury individual as you, that's all.'

'Really?' He smiled, but it was just a twist of the hard carved lips. 'And what have you decided?'

She glared at him for one moment more, her blue eyes sparking with the force of her emotion, and then turned and began walking up the road, trying not to limp in spite of the excruciating pain in her ankle, which seemed worse now she had rested it for a few moments.

She heard the engine rev behind her and fully expected the big vehicle to roar past her in a flurry of snow, so when it drew up beside her, keeping pace with her limping gait, she bit her lip hard but didn't turn her head from the white landscape in front of her.

'You said you fell over and twisted your ankle,' the hateful voice said flatly at the side of her.

She ignored it, along with the urge to burst into tears as waves of self-pity made themselves known.

'Get in.' This time the touch of raw impatience was very obvious, but again Marigold ignored him, struggling on, her face set resolutely ahead.

'Miss Jones, I think I ought to point out that you are extremely lucky I had an appointment elsewhere today which necessitated my leaving this morning. There is absolutely no chance of anyone else using this road and the cottage is at least another mile. Need I say more?' he added condescendingly.

'Get lost,' she bit out through gritted teeth.

There was a moment's pause and then his voice drawled, with disparaging amusement, 'Out of the two of us I would say that's a more likely occurrence for you. Get in the car, Miss Jones, and let's cut out the drama. It might be unpleasant for you to be told the truth for once, but you are old enough, and I'm sure tough enough, to survive.'

'I would rather freeze to death than accept a lift from you.' She turned for just an instant to meet the silvergrey eyes and her face spoke for itself.

'Now you are being ridiculous.'

'Well, that's just one more thing you can add to my list of crimes, then, isn't it?' she returned tartly.

'Get in the car.'

At this point Marigold so far forgot herself as to come out with an expletive she had never used in her life before. He thought he could order her about, tell her what to do after he had spoken to her the way he had? OK, so he might think she was Emma, and Marigold had to admit she didn't know all the ins and outs of this matter, but he had known she was asking for help and that she was hurt, and he had just left her standing in the snow while he'd given her a lecture on family responsibility. Nothing, but *nothing* would induce her to accept any form of assistance from this arrogant swine.

'Don't force me to make you get into the car, Miss Jones.'

'You think you could?' she spat derisively.

'Oh, yes.' It was cool and even and more than a little menacing, but the rage caused by his previous misplaced contempt and male arrogance was still hot enough to keep Marigold walking on, her head held high under its covering of wet plastic and the bottom of the cagoule flapping round her knees.

If he laid one finger on her, just one, he'd get a darn sight more than he'd bargained for, Marigold promised herself with silent fury as the vehicle drew level with her once again.

'Your grandmother was a woman in a million.'

Marigold ignored him completely.

'For her sake I don't intend to leave the only child of her son to freeze out here, even if it is exactly what you deserve.'

'How dare you?' She glared at him again, her eyes narrowed and shooting blue sparks but her lips were bloodless with the pain she was trying to conceal and her face was as white as a sheet. He stared at her for a second, the piercing eyes taking everything in, and then he sighed irritably before springing out of the vehicle with an abruptness which took Marigold by surprise. One moment she was standing glowering at him, the next she found herself whisked right off her feet as he lifted her up into his arms as though she weighed nothing at all.

'What on earth do you think you're playing at? Put

me down this instant!' she hissed furiously, struggling
violently as she pushed at the solid male chest.

'Keep still,' he muttered exasperatedly, striding round
the vehicle and depositing her in the passenger seat none
too gently. She immediately tried to scramble out again,
catching her injured foot as she did so and crying out
with pain before she could check the yelp.

'Miss Jones, I have a length of rope in the back and
I warn you I will have absolutely no compunction about
securing you in your seat, all right?' he ground out
tightly. 'You will sit there until we reach Maggie's cottage and then as far as I am concerned it'll be good
riddance to bad rubbish, and I'll have done my duty.'

'You're despicable!' It was all she could manage with
the pain now excruciating, but added to the physical dis-
comfort was the shock which had gripped her in the last
few moments. This man must be all of six feet four, and
his tall, lean height and powerfully muscled body had
convinced her she didn't have a hope of fighting him,
but close to—and she had been close, how close she
didn't dare dwell on right at this moment—he was ag-
gressively and compellingly handsome with no sign of
softness about him at all.

His face above the massive, thick oatmeal sweater he
wore was darkly tanned and finely chiselled, his eyes of
silver-grey ice set under black brows thrown into more
startling prominence when taken with the jet-black hair
falling over his forehead. He was...well, he was quite
amazing, Marigold thought weakly after he had slammed
the passenger door shut.

She watched him walk round the bonnet before he
climbed in the open driver's door, unconsciously shrink-
ing away slightly as he slid into the vehicle. If he noticed
the instinctive withdrawal he made no sign of it, merely

easing the car forward—the engine of which he had kept running—as he said, his voice curt, 'Did you arrange for food and fuel to be delivered to the cottage beforehand?'

No, because she hadn't known she could. Emma hadn't mentioned it when she'd offered her the use of the place over Christmas when Marigold had confided, a couple of weeks ago, that she was dreading the big family Christmas her parents always enjoyed. Their enormous, sprawling semi was always full of friends and relations over the holiday period right up until the new year—a kind of open house—which was great normally, but in view of her broken engagement and cancelled wedding was not so good. Everyone would be trying to be tactful and treading on eggshells. Poor, *poor* Marigold—that sort of thing.

'Why don't you tell them you've got the chance of a super little cottage with log fires and the full Christmas thing?' Emma had suggested after she'd offered the cottage and Marigold had said her parents would expect her to go home. 'I can understand they'd hate the thought of you staying in your flat by yourself, but if you say you and a friend are going away... And anyway, I'll be coming up a couple of days after Boxing Day to make a list of the furniture and one or two things, so it won't actually be a lie.'

Marigold thrust the reminder of her duplicity out of her thoughts as she answered the man at the side of her in as curt a tone as he had used, 'No, I didn't.'

'And when was the cottage used last?'

She didn't know that either. She thought quickly and then said airily, 'Recently.'

'Recently as in months or weeks?' he persisted coldly.

She wanted to tell him to mind his own business but in view of the present circumstances it seemed somewhat inappropriate. She remembered Emma had said the cottage might strike a bit cold and damp in the winter because she had only ever visited it in the warmer months, and guessed, 'Months.'

He nodded but said nothing more, concentrating on the road ahead, which was nothing but a cloud of whirling snowflakes in a landscape that was now a winter wonderland when viewed from the comforting warmth and security of the powerful car. Marigold privately admitted to a feeling of overpowering relief that she wasn't still battling through what was fast becoming a blizzard, and along with the acknowledgement came a few pangs of guilt at her churlishness before she reminded herself that *she* shouldn't feel guilty! He had been way, *way* out of line to talk to her as he had—even if he did believe she was Emma, and however much he had liked and respected the old lady. Rushing in and assuming this and that!

She risked a sidelong glance under her long lashes, aware she was dripping water all over the seat and that the melted snow from her boots had created a pool at her feet.

His face was hard, as though it had been carved from solid rock; he didn't seem quite human. Marigold suddenly became aware she was completely at this fierce stranger's mercy and she swallowed deeply. Somehow the idea of a noisy, crowded Christmas ensconced in the womb of her parents' home didn't seem so bad.

'Don't look so nervous; I wouldn't touch Maggie's granddaughter with a bargepole in case you're harbouring thoughts of rape and pillage.'

The deep voice had a thread of amusement running through it and immediately it put steel in Marigold's backbone. She reared up in her seat, her face, which had been pale a moment ago, now flushed with high colour, and her voice sharp as she lied, 'Nothing was further from my thoughts.'

'Hmm.' It was just one low grunt but carried a wealth of disbelief.

Loathsome man! Marigold drew her usually soft, full lips into a tight line and warned herself not to respond to the taunt. In a little while she would be at the cottage and he would be gone. She could see about bathing her ankle and strapping it up, and then she would sort herself out for the night. This snowstorm wouldn't last forever, and come morning she could make her way back to Myrtle and see if the little car could be persuaded to start. If not...well, she'd just have to carry everything to the cottage herself somehow. She didn't dwell on the thought of how she was going to lug her suitcase and the bags of food, let alone the sack of coal and other things she'd brought with her, through deep snow with an ankle that was hurting more every minute and now so swollen she wondered how she was going to get her boot off.

Nor did she linger on the fact that if the snow continued to fall as it was doing, two inches could rapidly become two feet. Coping with this angry, aggressive individual at the side of her was more than enough for the moment.

The ground had been dipping downwards almost from the spot where she'd first heard the car, and now, as they turned a corner on the winding road, Marigold saw they were in a wooded valley and that to their left in the distance was what must be Emma's cottage. It was set back some fifty yards from the track in its own garden, complete with neat picket fence and small gate. The cottage itself was painted white, from what Marigold could see, and it was the slate roof which was most clearly visible through the swirling snow.

She breathed a silent sigh of relief and gingerly flexed her injured ankle, knowing she had to climb out of the vehicle and walk to the cottage door in a few moments. The immediate stab of white-hot pain was worrying, but again she told herself it would be all right once she could strap it up.

'Your inheritance.' It was caustic.

She turned her head and looked at the granite profile. 'What makes you think it might be put on the market?' she asked evenly.

'Well, apart from the fact that you and the rest of your family have already shown you have no soul, you were heard talking about it in the pub down the road when you came up before,' he said shortly.

'People *eavesdropped* on a private conversation and then had the gall to repeat it?' Marigold asked with genuine disgust.

Her tone evidently rattled him. 'From what I heard, this "private" conversation was all but yelled to the rafters after you and your partner had consumed a bottle of wine each. If you don't want people to overhear what you say, don't get drunk. You can perhaps moderate your voice better that way. And the comments about the "yokels" didn't win you any friends in these parts either,' he added scathingly.

Oh, Emma, Marigold winced inwardly. She'd known Emma for a little while, but since she had met her current boyfriend—a high-flier with a sports car and a big opinion of himself—she'd changed.

Fortunately the car had just pulled up outside the little garden gate and Marigold was saved the effort of having to think of a reply. She took a deep breath and prayed this could end right now and that she would never set eyes on this man again in the whole of her life. 'Thank you for giving me a lift,' she said stiffly, conscious of the drips of water trickling off the cagoule hood and hitting her nose.

'A pleasure,' he drawled with heavy sarcasm, un-hooking her knapsack, which had somehow managed to jam itself to one side of the controls, after which he opened his door and walked round the bonnet to open her door for her.

The courtesy surprised her, especially in view of the content of their conversation to date, and flustered her still more, highlighting, as it did, the dark attractiveness she had been trying to ignore for the last few minutes. She would have liked to ignore the outstretched hand, too, but in view of the pain in her ankle and the height of the car she decided to err on the side of caution as she rose, putting her weight onto her good foot.

She had stripped off her wet gloves in the car, stuffing them in her pocket, and now as she put one small naked paw into his large fingers the contact of skin on skin brought an unwelcome little tingle of awareness in her flesh. She hesitated for a second, wondering how she was going to land on her injured ankle and whether she should try and shift her weight onto it now so she could land on her good foot.

'How bad is the ankle feeling?' he asked flatly.

He had obviously noticed her uncertainty and guessed the reason for it, and, in her immediate desire to convince this brute of a man that she was *perfectly* all right and didn't need his assistance a second longer, Marigold did what she later admitted to herself was a very silly thing. She stepped down from the vehicle, hoping her

ankle would support her for the brief time it took for her
to bring her other foot to bear. It didn't, of course.

She lunged sideways, the pain unbearable for a few
sickening moments, and because he still had hold of her
hand she swung like a plastic-wrapped rag doll on the
end of his arm, her hood falling off her hair as she
twisted against him. He almost overbalanced, too, saving
himself just in time and gathering her against him in
seconds as he half lifted her against his hard male frame.

Marigold had always bewailed the straight, sleek silk-
iness of her hair, which utterly refused to allow itself to
be curled or put up in elegant, sophisticated styles, but
now as the rich chestnut veil swung over her hot face
she was immensely glad of the thick, concealing screen.
Her reluctant good Samaritan was swearing under his
breath, but then, as the world steadied and righted itself
and his voice died away, she nerved herself to flick back
her tousled hair and look at him.

He was looking at her too and his face was just inches
away. Close to, his lips appeared more sensuous than
hard, she found herself thinking—totally inappropri-
ately—and the lines carved into the tanned skin radiating
from his eyes and his mouth added a depth to the good
looks he wouldn't have had in his teens and early manhood. And his eyelashes; she hadn't realised how long
and thick they were—utterly wasted on a man.

Marigold felt her nerve-ends begin to prickle and it
was the subtle sexual warning that enabled her to draw
back in his arms, forcing more space between them, as
she said breathlessly, 'I'm all right now, really. I'm
sorry, I just lost my footing…'

'Can you walk?' His eyes had moved to her hair and
then back to the wide violet eyes, and there was a smoky
quality to his voice which hadn't been there before. It

caused the most peculiar sensations to flutter down every nerve and sinew.

'Yes, yes...' She tried to prove it by pulling free and hobbling a step, but found to her dismay that the brief period of inactivity in the car had made the ankle feel ten times worse, not better.

As her lips went white with the pain he swore again, lifting her right off her feet with the same effortless strength he had shown on the road. She was being held close to the broad masculine chest for the second time in as many minutes, and she found it more than a little surreal as he strode over to the gate, kicking it open with scant regard for Emma's property and striding up the snow-covered path towards the front door.

He didn't glance down at her again until they reached the door, and then he said crisply, 'Key?'

'What?' She had seen his lips move and heard the sound but somehow the word hadn't registered in her brain. She was conscious of being held by him, of the leashed power in the hard male frame next to her and the subtle and delicious smell of his aftershave, and everything else seemed to have faded to the perimeter of her awareness.

'The key. For the door.' It was said with a derisive patience that brought her out of the stupor more effectively than a bucket of cold water.

'Oh, yes, of course.' She knew she was as red as a beetroot. 'You...you'll have to put me down. It's in my pocket and I can't reach it.'

'Stand on one foot; I'll hold you. And don't try to walk until we've taken a look at that ankle.'

We? *We?* If her pulse hadn't been thudding so crazily and her throat hadn't been so strangely dry she might have challenged him on the 'we', but as it was she assumed a pose she had seen the pink flamingos adopt in a recent wildlife documentary as he lowered her gently down, and fumbled for the key. She was horribly conscious of his hands round her waist, and although she told herself he was only steadying her it didn't help.

The trouble was he was too *male* a man, she thought distractedly. It wasn't just that he was big, very big, but he was larger than life somehow. Very tall, very hard and handsome and muscled, very everything in fact. In the most disturbing and unnerving way.

'Here it is.'

He adjusted his stance slightly, sliding one arm round her, positioning her against his masculine thigh as he took the key from her nerveless fingers. It was ridiculous, truly ridiculous, she told herself feverishly, in view of all the layers of clothing between them, but it felt shatteringly intimate.

As the door swung open he picked her up again and stepped into a small square hall, clicking on a light switch to one side of the door as he did so. He obviously knew his way around the cottage, Marigold thought, and this was borne out in the next moment when he opened a door to their right and entered what was clearly the sitting room, turning on the light again as he did so. The room was crowded with old, heavy furniture, smelt fusty and damp and had an unlived-in air which was chilling in itself as he placed her on a sofa in front of an empty fireplace.

It was awful. Marigold cast despairing eyes over her temporary home. Absolutely awful. And so *cold*. And no doubt the bedroom was just as damp and chilly. Whatever was she going to do? She looked sideways at the man standing to one side of the sofa and saw he was looking at her in an uncomfortably speculative way.

'Lovely,' she said brightly. 'Well, I think I can manage perfectly well now, thank you, and I'm sure you want to get home—'

'Sit still while I light a fire; the place is like a damn fridge. We'll attend to the ankle in a moment.'

He had disappeared out of the door before she could bring her startled mind to order, and as she heard another door open and close she called desperately, 'Mr Moreau? Please, I can manage now. I would much prefer to be left alone. Mr Moreau? Can you hear me?'

It was a minute or two before he returned, and then with a face as black as thunder. 'There's no coal or wood in the storehouse,' he said accusingly. 'Did you know?'

She could have told him it was because Emma and Oliver had had coal fires every night when they'd been here—despite it having been high summer. 'So romantic, darling,' Emma had cooed. 'And Oliver just loves to enter into the whole country thing.'

Instead she just nodded before saying, 'There's some in my car.'

'But your car isn't here,' he ground out slowly.

'I can see to it in the morning.'

He shut his eyes for a moment as though he couldn't believe his ears, before opening them and pinning her with his gaze as he said, 'Ye gods, woman! This isn't the centre of London, you know. There's not a garage on every other corner.'

'I'm well aware of that,' Marigold said as haughtily as she could; the effect being ruined somewhat by her chattering teeth. 'I'm hoping Myrtle will be all right tomorrow.'

The eagle eyes narrowed, a slightly bemused expression coming over his dark face. 'One of us is losing the plot here,' he murmured in a rather self-derisory tone. 'Who the hell is Myrtle?'

Marigold could feel her face flooding with colour. 'My car.'

'Your car. Right.' He took a long, deep and very visible pull of air, letting it out slowly before he said, in an insultingly long-suffering voice, 'And if...Myrtle decides not to fall in with your plans, what then? And how are you going to walk on that foot? And what are you going to do for heat tonight?'

Marigold decided to just answer the last question; of the three he'd posed it seemed the safest. 'Tonight I'm just planning on a hot drink and then bed,' she said stoutly.

'I see.' He was standing with his legs slightly apart and his arms crossed, a pose which emphasised his brooding masculinity, and from her perch on the sofa he seemed bigger than ever in the crowded little room. 'Let me show you something.'

Before she could object he'd bent down and picked her up again—it was getting to be a habit to be in his arms, Marigold thought a trifle hysterically as he marched out of the sitting room and into the room next to it. This was clearly the bedroom and boasted its own share of clutter in the way of a huge old wardrobe, ancient dressing table and chest of drawers, two dilapidated large cane chairs with darned cushions and a stout and substantial bed with a carved wooden headboard. If anything this struck damper and chillier than the sitting room.

'That mattress will need airing for hours even if you use your own sheets and blankets,' he said grimly. 'Did you bring your own?'

He looked down at her as he spoke and she felt the

impact of the beautiful silver-grey eyes in a way that took her breath away.

This man was dangerous, she thought suddenly. Dangerous to any woman's peace of mind. He had a sexual magnetism that was stronger than the earth's magnetic field, and she'd sensed it even when he was being absolutely horrible on the road earlier. And he was ruthless; it was there in the harshly sculpted mouth and classic cheekbones, along with the square, determined thrust to his chin and the piercing intensity of his eyes. The sooner he left the more comfortable she'd feel.

'Well?'

Too late Marigold realised she'd been staring up at him like a mesmerised rabbit, and now she shook her head quickly, her cheeks flushing. 'No, Em—I mean, I didn't think I'd need any with there being bedding here,' she said quickly as he turned abruptly, striding through to the sitting room, whereupon he deposited her on the sofa again.

'Your grandmother kept a fire burning in the sitting room and bedroom day and night from October to May,' he said flatly, 'and the cottage was always as warm as toast when she was alive. But this is an old place with solid walls; not a centrally heated, cavity-walled little city box.'

He was being nasty again; his tone was caustic. Marigold tried to summon up the requisite resentment and anger but it was hard with her body still registering the feel and smell of him. 'Be that as it may, I'll be fine, Mr Moreau,' she managed fairly firmly. 'I noticed one of those old stone bed warmers on the chest of drawers in the other room; I'll air the bed with that tonight and—'

'There's nothing else for it. You'll have to come back

home with me.' He didn't seem to be aware she'd been
talking.

As a gracious invitation it was a non-starter; his voice
couldn't have been more irritated, but it wasn't his obvious distaste of the thought of having her as a guest
which made Marigold say, and quickly, 'Thank you but
I wouldn't dream of it,' but the lingering, traitorous response of her body to his closeness.

'This is not a polite social suggestion, Miss Jones, but
a necessity,' he bit out coldly. 'Now personally I'd be
happy to leave you here to freeze to death or worse, but
I know Maggie wouldn't have wanted that.'

'I shan't freeze to death,' she snapped back.

'You have no heat, no food—'

'I've a couple of tins of baked beans and a loaf of
bread in my knapsack,' she interrupted triumphantly.

The expression in the crystal eyes spoke volumes. 'No
heat and no food,' he repeated sternly, 'and you can't
even walk on two feet. You've obviously damaged your
ankle severely enough for it to be a problem for a few
days, and without fuel and food your stay here is untenable.'

'It is *not* untenable!' She couldn't believe the way he
was riding roughshod over her. 'I've told you—'

'That you have two tins of baked beans and a loaf of
bread. Yes, I know.' It was the height of sarcasm and
she could have cheerfully hit him. 'Let me make one
thing clear, Miss Jones. You are coming with me, will-
ingly or unwillingly; of your own volition or tied up like
a sack of potatoes. It's all the same to me. I shall send
someone to see to the car and also to start getting the
cottage warm and aired; believe me, I have as little wish
for your company as you seem to have for mine. Once

we've ascertained the extent of the damage to your ankle we can consider when you can return here.'

And it couldn't be soon enough for him. Marigold stared up into the cold, angry face in front of her, reminding herself it was Emma he was furious at—Emma and her family. And if they had neglected the old lady as he suggested he probably had good cause for his disgust, she admitted, but he was a hateful, *hateful* pig of a man and she loathed him. Oh, how she loathed him.

'So, what's it to be? With your consent or trussed up like a Christmas turkey?' he asked in such a way she just knew he was hoping for the latter.

She glared at him, almost speechless. Almost. 'You are easily the most unpleasant individual I have ever come across in my life,' she said furiously.

Her smouldering expression seemed to amuse him if anything. 'I repeat, Miss Jones, are you coming quietly and at least pretending to be a lady or—?'

'I'll come,' she spat with soft venom.

'And very gratefully accepted,' he drawled pleasantly, his good humour apparently fully restored.

She eyed him balefully as she struggled to her feet, pushing aside his hand when he reached out to help her. 'I can manage, thank you, and don't you dare try and manhandle me again,' she snapped testily.

'Manhandle you? I thought I was assisting a…lady in distress,' he said mockingly, the deliberate pause before the word 'lady' bringing new colour surging into Marigold's cheeks. 'How are you going to walk out to my car?'

'I'll hop,' she determined darkly.

And she did.

CHAPTER TWO

'So, MISS JONES, or can I call you Emma, as you have so graciously consented to be a house guest?' They had just driven away from the cottage and the snow was coming down thicker than ever, Marigold noted despairingly. She nodded abruptly to his enquiry, earning herself a wry sidelong glance. 'And you must call me Flynn.'

Must she? She didn't think so. And there was a perverse satisfaction in knowing he didn't have a clue who she really was.

'So why, Emma, have you decided to spend Christmas at your grandmother's cottage and all alone by the look of it? From what I've heard from your grandmother and more especially from the ''yokels'' after your last visit, it just isn't your style. What's happened to the yuppie boyfriend?'

Oliver *was* a yuppie, and Marigold couldn't stand him, but hearing Flynn Moreau refer to the other man in a supercilious tone suddenly made Oliver a dear friend!

Marigold forced a disdainful shrug. 'My reasons are my own, surely?' she said coolly.

He nodded cheerfully, not at all taken aback by the none-too subtle rebuke. 'Sure, and hey, there'll be no objections from anyone hereabouts that lover boy's not with you,' he added with charming malice. 'He didn't exactly win any friends when he swore at the landlord and then argued about the bill for your meal.'

Oh, wonderful. Emma and Oliver had certainly made an impression all right, a bad one! Marigold sighed inwardly. Her ankle was throbbing unbearably, she didn't have so much as a nightie with her, and it was Christmas Eve the day after tomorrow; a Christmas Eve which Dean and Tamara would spend under a hot Caribbean sky, locked in each other's arms most likely.

She wasn't aware her mouth had drooped, or that she appeared very small and very vulnerable, buried in the enormous cagoule with her shoulder-length hair slightly damp and her hands tightly clasped in her lap, so it came as something of a surprise when a quiet voice said, 'Don't worry. My housekeeper will look after you once we reach Oaklands and her husband can take a load of logs and coal to the cottage tonight and begin drying it out. He's something of an expert with cars, too, so Myrtle might respond to his tender touch.'

Marigold glanced at Flynn warily. The sudden transformation from avenging angel breathing fire and brimstone to understanding human being was suspect, and her face must have spoken for itself because he gave a small laugh, low in his throat. 'I don't bite,' he said softly. 'Well, not little girls anyway.'

'I'm a grown woman of twenty-five, thank you,' she responded quickly, although her voice wasn't as sharp as she would have liked. Hateful and argumentative he had been disturbing; quiet and comforting he was doubly so. When she had been fighting him she had felt safer; now she was on shifting ground and the chemical reaction he had started in her body before was even stronger.

'Twenty-five?' Dark brows frowned. 'I thought Maggie sent you a present for your twenty-first just before she died?'

Oops. Marigold decided to bluff it out. 'I can assure

you, I know how old I am,' she answered tartly, and then, seeing he was about to say more, she added quickly, 'Is Oaklands your house?'

He didn't reply for a moment, and then he nodded. 'I bought it from a friend of mine who decided to emigrate to Canada a couple of years ago,' he said shortly. 'Your grandmother might have spoken of him; apparently they were great friends. Peter Lyndon?'

Marigold nodded vaguely and hoped that would do.

'She missed him when he left,' Flynn continued quietly. 'His children used to come across the valley and visit her often and they were a substitute for her real family, I suppose.' The accusing note was back but Marigold chose to ignore it. 'Certainly when I called to see her it was photographs of Peter's family that she showed me. She never showed me any of yours—too painful probably.'

Marigold felt she ought to object here. 'How can you say that when you have just admitted you didn't know her very long?' she asked in as piqued a voice as she could manage, considering all her sympathies—had he but known it—were with Emma's poor grandmother. The family seemed to have behaved appallingly to the old woman, and although as a work acquaintance Emma was perfectly pleasant it wasn't beyond the bounds of possibility to imagine her disregarding the fact she'd got a grandmother if it suited her to do so.

'Peter was a good deal older than me and he'd known Maggie for a long time,' Flynn said evenly. 'I think he knew your father, too. They didn't get on.' There was a pregnant pause.

Again Marigold felt she ought to say something. 'I don't know anything about that,' she said truthfully, and then she stopped abruptly, aware they were passing through large open gates set in a six-foot dry-stone wall which had appeared suddenly out of the thick cloud of snow in front of them. This must be the grounds of his home.

The car was travelling along a drive flanked by enormous oak trees, stark and beautiful in their winter mantle of feathery white, and she could just make out a house in the distance. A very large, very grand house. Marigold swallowed hard as Emma's casual comment about the other dwelling in the valley came back to her—a manor house. And this was a manor house all right.

She glanced speculatively at Flynn under her eyelashes; the expensive and clearly nearly new vehicle, the thick, beautifully cut leather jacket she'd noticed slung in the back seat, the overall quality of his clothes suddenly making an impression on her buzzing senses. Her eyes moved to the large tanned hands on the steering wheel—was that a designer watch on one wrist? It was. A beauty. Oh, boy... Marigold stifled a groan. This guy was *loaded*.

A couple of enormous long-haired German shepherd dogs suddenly appeared from nowhere, barking madly and making Marigold jump. 'Sorry, I should have warned you.' Flynn was looking straight ahead but he must have noticed her involuntary movement. 'That's Jake and Max; they pretend to be guard dogs.'

'Pretend?' Marigold looked out of the window at the enormous faces with even more enormous teeth staring up at her, and shivered. 'They've convinced me.'

Flynn turned and grinned at her as he brought the car to a halt, the dogs still leaping about the vehicle. 'Don't tell anyone but they sleep in front of the range in the kitchen,' he said softly, 'and they're scared stiff of my housekeeper's cats.'

Marigold managed a smile of her own but it was a weak one. Did he know what sort of effect the softening of the hard planes and angles of his face produced? she asked herself silently. It was dynamite. Sheer dynamite. 'I…I've never had much to do with dogs,' she said weakly.

And then his face changed. 'I'd gathered that,' he said shortly.

Now what had she said? Marigold stared at him uncomprehendingly. 'I'm sorry…?'

'It was made plain through the solicitors that any animals Maggie had were to be got rid of, but then you're aware of that,' Flynn said coldly, 'aren't you? Sold if anything could be got for them; put down if not. Of course, there weren't too many buyers for a few scruffy chickens and an ancient cow, nor for her dog and cat.'

Oh, no. Emma hadn't…

'Don't tell me that was something else your father kept from you?' Flynn asked flatly, his eyes smoky dark now in the muted twilight.

'I…I didn't know.'

'No?' His eyes were holding hers and she couldn't look away. 'I don't know if I believe that.'

Marigold had suddenly decided she didn't like Emma's family at all and was heartily wishing she hadn't taken the cottage for Christmas, even if she was paying Emma well for the privilege. 'I didn't know,' she repeated weakly, her tone unconvincing even to herself, but she was still thinking of poor Maggie's pets.

He surveyed her for a moment more, and Marigold was just about to tell him everything—that she wasn't Emma, that she had taken the cottage on impulse when it was offered and only knew the barest facts about Emma and her grandmother and the family—when he shrugged coolly. 'It's history now,' he said evenly. 'Let's get you inside.'

As she watched him walk round the bonnet of the car the fate of the animals was lost in the panic that he was going to hold her again. She'd felt faintness wash over her a couple of times when she had hopped out to the car, the movement jarring her injured ankle unbearably, but right now that was preferable to being held next to that muscled body again. Being nestled close to his chest had caused a reaction inside she still couldn't come to terms with.

She had never responded to a man's body or presence like this before, not with Dean, not with anyone, and her brain was still reeling from the unwelcome knowledge that underneath the panic and alarm was forbidden pleasure. Pleasure and excitement.

She would tell him she could hop into the house, she decided as he came towards the door. It wasn't quite the entrance she would have wished for, what with his housekeeper and her husband watching—not to mention the two dogs with their slavering jaws—but it couldn't be helped. What did it matter about a little lost dignity or the dogs thinking her dangling leg was a new toy?

As it happened, Flynn didn't give her the chance to make her feelings known one way or the other. The car door was pulled open and she was in his arms in the next moment and being carried towards the front door of the house, which was now open, the dogs gambolling about them and barking madly at this new game and Flynn swearing at them under his breath.

The lady who had opened the front door met them on the second step, her plump, plain face concerned as she said, 'Oh, Mr Moreau, whatever's happened?'

'I'll explain inside.'

And what an inside. As the warmth of the house hit Marigold, so did the opulence of the surroundings. The entrance hall was all wooden floors and expensive rugs and a wide, gracious staircase that went up and up into infinity, passing galleried landings as it did so.

However, she only had time for one bemused glance before she was carried into what was obviously the drawing room, and placed on a deep, soft sofa which had been pulled close to the blazing log fire. One arm had been round Flynn's neck, and although he had held her quite impersonally every nerve in her body was vitally and painfully alive and for a crazy second—a ridiculous, *insane* second—she had wondered what he'd do if she'd tightened her hold on him and pulled his mouth down to hers. It had been enough to keep her as rigid as a plank of wood when he'd lowered her carefully onto the sofa.

'This is Miss Jones, Bertha.' Flynn turned to the housekeeper, who had been right behind them. 'Maggie's granddaughter. Her car broke down a mile or so from the cottage and she's hurt her ankle. Take care of her, would you, while I find Wilf and tell him to go and take a look at the car? He can take John with him; I'd like them to get it back here if possible. And we've got a few spare electric heaters dotted about the place, haven't we? They can take those and start warming the cottage. And get John to deliver a load of logs and a few sacks of coal tomorrow morning.'

'Please, it's not necessary...' She had to tell them she wasn't Emma. She didn't know now why she hadn't told Flynn before, except that it had suited something deep inside to let him make a fool of himself when he had been so obnoxious on the road at first. And then she'd felt backed into a corner somehow, and there had never seemed to be a suitable moment to confess the truth. But this was getting more embarrassing, more awful, by the minute.

Flynn was already walking towards the door when Marigold said urgently, 'Mr Moreau? Please, I need to explain—'

'First things first.' He turned in the doorway, his face unsmiling and his voice cool. 'I need to get Wilf and John along to the car before it's completely dark, and you need that foot seen to. And the name's Flynn, as I told you before.'

'But you don't understand…' Her voice stopped abruptly. He had gone. Marigold looked up at the housekeeper, who was peering down at her over her apron, and said dazedly, 'I need to talk to him.'

'All in good time, lovey. You look like you've been in the wars, if I may say so. Now, let's get your things off and then we'll try and ease that boot off your poorly foot, all right? I'll be as careful as I can but I reckon we might have a bit of a job with it if your ankle's swollen.'

At least there was *someone* who didn't think she was horrible, Marigold thought gratefully as she returned the older woman's friendly smile. And after the last hour or so that felt wonderful.

In the event they had to cut the wellington boot off her foot, and when her ankle was displayed in all its glory the housekeeper drew the air in between her teeth in a soft hiss before saying, 'Oh, dear. Oh, dear, oh, dear, oh, dear. You've done a job on that, lovey.'

'It will be all right.' Nothing was going to keep Marigold in the house a second longer than was absolutely necessary. 'Once it's strapped up and after a good night's rest I'll be fine.'

The housekeeper shook her grey head doubtfully as

she looked at the puffy red and blue flesh, and then bustled off to get two bowls of hot and cold water—'to bring the bruise out', she informed Marigold before she left.

Marigold thought it was coming out pretty well all on its own. She lay back on the sofa, her foot now propped on a leather pouffe, and shut her eyes, trying to ignore the sickening pain in her foot. What a pickle, she thought despairingly. She was an unwelcome guest in the home of a man who loathed her—or loathed the person he thought she was at least—and if she wasn't careful she'd impose on him over Christmas. But she wouldn't, no matter how her ankle was tomorrow, she promised herself fervently. She'd make sure she went to the cottage tomorrow if she had to crawl every inch of the way. But it was going to be a pretty miserable Christmas by the look of it. At least she'd had the foresight to call her parents from a big old-fashioned red phone box at the side of the road just after the pub, and let them know she was within a few miles of the cottage and that she was all right but that she wouldn't be calling them again.

Once she'd got herself sorted at the cottage she could sit in front of the fire and read Christmas away while she nursed her ankle. There were people in much worse situations than she was in, and she had plenty of food in the car, and now she was going to have an excess of fuel by the sound of it. She'd pay him for the logs and coal, and his trouble, she thought firmly. If nothing else she could do that. And thank him. She twisted uncomfortably on the sofa, more with the realisation that she hadn't even acknowledged his—albeit reluctant and grudging—kindness in offering her sanctuary for the night.

'When Bertha said it was bad, she meant it was bad.'

Marigold's eyes shot open as she jerked upright. Flynn had reappeared as quietly as a cat and was now standing surveying her through narrowed silver eyes. For a moment she thought he was going to be sympathetic or at least compliment her on her stoicism, but she was swiftly disabused of this pleasant notion when he continued, his tone irate, 'What the hell were you thinking of, trying to walk on it once you'd hurt yourself so badly? Didn't you realise you were making it a hundred times worse with each step, you stupid girl?'

'Now, look—' a moment ago she'd been feeling weak and pathetic; now there was fire running through her veins '—I didn't know you were going to come along, did I? What was I supposed to do? Hobble back to the car and freeze to death or try and reach the cottage where there was—?'

'Absolutely no heat or food,' he cut in nastily. 'And why didn't you try phoning someone anyway? Anyone! The emergency services, for example. Do you have emergency insurance?'

'Yes.' It was a snap.

'But you didn't think of asking for help? It was easier to march off into the blizzard like Scott in the Antarctic?'

She bit hard on her lip. He was just going to love this! 'I'd left my mobile at home,' she admitted woodenly.

He said nothing at all to this—he didn't have to. His face spoke volumes.

'And my ankle's not that bad anyway,' she added tightly.

'It's going to be twice the size it is now in the morning and all the colours of the rainbow,' he said quietly.

The cool diagnosis irritated her. 'How do you know?' she returned churlishly. 'You're not a doctor.'

'Actually I am.' She blinked at him, utterly taken aback, and the carved lips twitched a little at her amazement.

The knowledge that he was laughing at her brought out the worst in Marigold, and now she said, in a tone which even she recognised as petulant, 'Oh, really? A brain surgeon or something, I suppose?'

'Right.'

Her eyes widened to blue saucers. Oh, he wasn't, was he? Not a neurosurgeon? He couldn't be!

She said as much, but when he still continued to survey her steadily and his face didn't change expression she knew he wasn't joking. And of course he couldn't have been a normal doctor, could he? she asked herself acidly. A nice, friendly GP dealing with all the trials and tribulations that the average man, woman and child brought his way. Someone who was overworked and underpaid and who had a vast list of patients demanding his attention.

She knew she was being massively unfair. She knew it, but where this particular individual was concerned she just couldn't *help* it.

She forced herself to say, and pleasantly, 'Not your average nine-to-five, then?'

'Not quite.' He was still watching her intently.

'Do you work from a hospital near here or—?'

'London. I have a flat there.'

Well, he would have, wouldn't he? Marigold nodded in what she hoped appeared an informed sort of way. 'It must be very rewarding to help people...' Her words were cut off in a soft gasp as he knelt down in front of her, taking her foot in his large hands—hands with long, slim fingers and clean fingernails, she noted faintly, surgeon's hands—and gently rotating it in his grasp as he felt the bruised flesh. How gently she wouldn't have believed if she hadn't felt it. Suddenly his occupation was perfectly feasible.

She wanted to snatch her foot away but in the state it was in that wasn't an option. She glanced down at the thick, jet-black hair which shone with blue lights and found herself saying, 'Moreau... That's not English, is it?'

'French.' He raised his eyes from her foot and Marigold's heart hammered in her chest. 'My father was French-Italian and my mother was American-Irish but they settled in England before I was born.'

'Quite a mixture,' she managed fairly lucidly because he had now placed her foot back on the pouffe and stood to his feet again and wasn't actually touching her any more.

Bertha bustled in with the basins of water and a towel draped over one arm, and Flynn glanced at his housekeeper as he turned and walked to the door. 'Five minutes alternating hot and cold, Bertha, and then I'll be back to strap it.'

He was as good as his word. Bertha had been making small talk while she bathed the ankle and Marigold had been relaxed and chatting quite easily, but the moment the big, tall figure appeared in the doorway she felt her stomach muscles form themselves into a giant knot and her voice become stilted as she thanked the housekeeper for her efforts.

As Bertha bustled away with the bowls of water Flynn walked across to the sofa. 'Take these.' He held out two small white tablets with a glass of water.

'What are they?' she asked tentatively.

'Poison.' And at her frown he added irritably, 'What do you think they are, for crying out loud? Pain relief.'

'I don't like taking tablets,' she said firmly.

'I don't like having to prescribe them but this is not a perfect world and sometimes they're necessary. Like now. Take them.'

'I'd rather not if you don't mind.'

'I do mind. You are going to be in considerable pain tonight with that foot and you won't get any sleep at all if you don't help yourself.'

'But—'

'Just take the damn tablets!'

He'd shouted, he'd actually shouted, Marigold thought with shocked surprise. He didn't have much of a bedside manner. She took the tablets.

Along with the tablets and water, the tray he was holding contained ointment and bandages, and she steeled herself for his touch as he kneeled down in front of her again. His fingers were deft and sure and sent flickering *frissons* radiating all over her body which made her as tight and tense as piano wire. And angry with herself. She couldn't understand how someone she had disliked on sight, and who was the last word in arrogance, could affect her so radically. It was humiliating.

'You should start to feel better in a minute or two,' Flynn said dispassionately as he rose to his feet, having completed his task.

'What?' For an awful minute she thought he had read her mind and was referring to the fact that he wasn't touching her any more, before common sense kicked in and she realised his words had been referring to the pain-killers and the support now easing her ankle. 'Oh, yes, thank you,' she said quickly.

'I'll get Bertha to bring you a hot drink and a snack.' He was standing in front of the sofa, looking at her steadily, and she could read nothing from his face. 'Then

I suggest you lie back and have a doze until dinner at eight. You must be exhausted,' he added impersonally.

She stared at him. He seemed to have gone into ice-man mode again after shouting at her and she rather thought she preferred it when he was yelling. Like this he was extremely intimidating. 'Thank you,' she said again, as there was really nothing else to say.

'You're welcome.'

She rather doubted that but she didn't say so. In truth she was feeling none too good and the thought of a nap was very appealing.

Flynn turned and walked to the door, stopping at the threshold to say, 'You've got severe bruising on the ankle, by the way; you'll be lucky to be walking normally within a couple of weeks.'

'A couple of weeks!' Marigold stared at him, horrified.

'You were very fortunate not to break a bone.'

Fortunate was not the word she would have used to describe her present circumstances, Marigold thought hotly as she protested, 'I'll be able to hobble about if I'm careful tomorrow, I'm sure. It feels better already now you've strapped it up.'

He said nothing for a moment although her remark had brought a twisted smile to his strong, sensual mouth. Then he drawled, 'Fortunately I think we have a pair of crutches somewhere or other; a legacy of last summer, when Bertha was unfortunate enough to have a nasty fall and dislocate her knee.'

Oh, right. So when Bertha hurt herself it was just an unfortunate accident; when *she* hurt herself it was because she was stupid! Marigold breathed deeply and then said sweetly, 'And I could borrow them for a while?'

'No problem.'

'Thank you.'

He nodded and walked out, shutting the door behind him, and it was only at that moment that Marigold realised she'd missed the perfect opportunity to set the record straight and explain who she really was.

CHAPTER THREE

AFTER eating the toasted sandwich and drinking the mug of hot chocolate Bertha brought her a few minutes after Flynn had left, Marigold must have fallen immediately asleep; her consuming tiredness due, no doubt, in part to the strong painkillers Flynn had given her.

She surfaced some time later to the sound of voices just outside the room, and for a moment, as she opened dazed eyes, she didn't know where she was. She stared into the glowing red and gold flames licking round the logs on the fire in the enormous stone fireplace vacantly, before a twinge in her ankle reminded her what had happened.

She pulled herself into a sitting position on the sofa, adjusting her foot on the pouffe as she did so, which brought forth more sharp stabs of pain, and she had just pulled down her waist-length cashmere jumper and adjusted the belt in her jeans, which had been sticking into her waist, when the door opened again.

The room was in semi-darkness, with just a large standard lamp in one corner competing with the glow from the huge fire, so when the main light was switched on Marigold blinked like a small, startled owl at Flynn and the other man. 'You'll be glad to know Myrtle is safe and snug and tucked up in one of the garages for the night,' Flynn said evenly as the two men walked across to the sofa. 'This is Wilf, by the way. Wilf, meet Miss Jones, Maggie's granddaughter.'

'But she isn't.' Bertha's husband was a small man

with a ruddy complexion and bright black robin eyes, and these same eyes were now staring at Marigold in evident confusion.

'What?'

'This isn't the same woman who was in the pub that day; the one who was all over that yuppie type and then made such a song and dance about being charged too much when Arthur gave them the bill,' Wilf said bewilderedly, totally unaware he was giving Marigold one of the worst moments of her entire life.

'I can explain—'

Flynn cut across Marigold's feverish voice, his own like ice as he said, 'Perhaps you would like to introduce yourself, Miss…?'

Marigold took a hard pull of air, reflecting if she didn't love her parents so much she would hate them for giving her a name which had always been an acute embarrassment to her. 'My name's Marigold,' she said a little unsteadily. 'Marigold Flower.'

'You're joking.'

She wished she were. She wished she could have announced a name like Tamara Jaimeson. 'No,' she assured Flynn miserably as he looked down at her, his expression utterly cold. 'My name really is Marigold Flower. My mother…well, she's a little eccentric, I guess, and when she married a Flower and then had a little girl she thought it was too good a chance to miss. My father was just relieved I wasn't a son. She was going to call a boy Gromwell. They're lovely pure blue flowers that my mother had in her rock garden at the time…'

Marigold's voice trailed away. She had been gabbling; Wilf's slightly glassy-eyed stare told her so. Flynn's eyes, on the other hand, were rapier-sharp and boring into her head like twin lasers.

'I'm pleased to meet you and thank you for dealing with the car.' She extended a hand to Wilf, who bent down and shook it before moving a step backwards as though he was frightened she would bite.

'Perhaps you would be good enough to leave Miss…Flower and myself alone for a few minutes, Wilf, and inform Bertha we don't want to be interrupted?' Flynn said grimly, his gaze not leaving Marigold's hot face.

Wilf needed no second bidding; he was out of the room like a shot and Marigold envied him with all her heart. She watched the door close and then looked up at Flynn, who was still standing quite still and looking at her steadily; the sort of look that made her feel she'd just crawled out from under a stone. 'I did try to tell you,' she muttered quickly before he said anything. 'Several times.'

'The hell you did.'

'I did!' She glared at him. Attack might not always be the best line of defence but it was all she had right now. 'But you blazed in, all guns firing, on the road before I even had a chance to open my mouth and wouldn't let me get a word in edgeways.'

'You're saying this is *my* fault?' he snarled in obvious amazement. 'You tell me a pack of lies, pretend to be someone else and inveigle your way into my home under false pretences—'

'I did not inveigle my way into your home,' she stormed furiously. 'I didn't want to come if you remember but you wouldn't take no for an answer, and I'll pay you for tonight and for the coal and logs. I can go to the cottage right now—'

She tried to rise too quickly and then fell back on the sofa with a shocked little cry, her face twisting with pain.

'For crying out loud, lie still!' He was shouting again and he seemed to realise this himself in the next instant. She watched him shut his eyes for an infinitesimal second before taking a great pull of air and letting it out harshly between his lips in a loud hiss. 'Lie still,' he said more quietly, the silver-grey eyes narrowed and cold and the muscles in his face clenching as he fought to gain control of himself.

Marigold had the feeling he didn't lose his temper all that often and that the fact that he had with her was another black mark against her. 'I *did* try to explain,' she said shakily, willing herself not to break down in front of this…this *monster*. 'But you wouldn't listen.'

He continued to survey her for what seemed like an eternity, before walking over to an exquisitely carved cocktail cabinet on the other side of the room near the massive bay windows, and pouring himself a stiff brandy. 'I would offer you one but you can't drink with those pills,' he said shortly. 'Would you like grapejuice, bitter lemon, tonic…?'

'A bitter lemon would be fine, thank you.' Marigold hoped the shaking in her stomach hadn't communicated itself in her voice, and whilst he was seeing to her drink she glanced round the room again. It was gorgeous, absolutely gorgeous, and everything in it just shouted wealth and influence and prestige. The ankle-deep cream carpet; the beautiful sofas and chairs in the palest of lavender mint, the colour reflected in a deeper shade in the long drapes at the windows; the rich dark wood of the bookcase and cocktail cabinet and occasional tables… Everything was beautiful.

'Here.' As Flynn handed her the drink she could read

nothing in his expressionless face, and after he had seated himself in an easy chair a few feet away he took a long swallow of the brandy before crossing one knee over the other and leaning back in his seat. 'I take it you *do* have permission to use the cottage?' he asked evenly.

'Of course,' she said indignantly, appalled he could think otherwise. 'I work with Emma.'

He nodded slowly, settling further back in the chair and continuing to look at her, obviously waiting for her to explain herself.

Marigold stared at him, wishing he wasn't so big, so male, so *irritatingly* sure of himself. But she *did* owe him an explanation, she admitted to herself silently. He had rescued her when all was said and done, and then brought her here, to his home. She took a deep breath and said steadily, 'I work with Emma, as I said, and she—'

'Doing what?' Flynn interrupted coolly.

'I beg your pardon?'

'You said you worked with her,' he said impatiently. 'In what capacity?'

'I'm a designer.' Marigold hesitated and then said quietly, 'Emma's the company's secretary. It's a small firm, just eight of us altogether, counting Patricia and Jeff, the two partners.'

'You enjoy your work?'

'Yes; yes, I do.'

At some point when she had been asleep Flynn had exchanged his thick sweater for a casual silk shirt in midnight-blue. It was buttoned to just below his collarbone, and in spite of herself Marigold's eyes were drawn to the smidgen of dark curling body hair just visible above the soft material. That, along with the very mas-

culine way he was sitting, made his aura of virile masculinity impossible to ignore.

Marigold gulped twice and went on, 'Anyway, Emma
offered me the cottage over Christmas a few days ago
and I accepted. It…it was all decided in a bit of a hurry,
I suppose.'

'Why?'

'Why?' She stared at him. 'Why what?'

'Why is someone as attractive as you spending
Christmas all alone? You can't tell me you didn't have
plenty of offers to the contrary,' he said expressionlessly.

It was a compliment of sorts, she supposed, although
his voice and his face were so cool and remote it didn't
feel like one. She didn't know quite how to answer for
a moment, and then she said carefully, 'Personal reasons.' She was grateful to him, she was really, but there
was no way she was going to give this arrogant, au-
thoritative stranger her life history.

'Ah…' He inclined his head and took a pull at the
brandy. The one word was incredibly irritating.

'Ah?' Marigold challenged immediately. 'What does
"ah" mean?'

He uncoiled his body, stretching lazily and finishing
the brandy in one gulp before saying, '"Ah" means you
are running away from a man.'

She had been having some trouble preventing her eyes
from following the line of his tight black jeans, but the
cynical and—more to the point—totally inaccurate statement was like a dose of icy water on her overwrought
nerves. 'I am *not*,' she declared angrily. How dared he
make such an assumption?

'No?'

'No.'

'But a man is at the bottom of this seclusion some-where.'

It was so arrogantly smooth she could have hit him, as much for being right as anything else. She could feel the hot colour in her cheeks, which had nothing to do with the roaring fire in the grate and everything to do with Flynn Moreau, and now her back was ramrod-straight as she glared at him, her mind frantically search-ing for an adequate put-down.

'You have a very expressive face.' Flynn stood up, not at all concerned about her fury. 'I should have known back there on the road you couldn't possibly be old Maggie's granddaughter.'

She didn't want to give Flynn the satisfaction of her asking the obvious but she found she couldn't help it. 'Why couldn't I be?' she asked tightly.

'Because from what Peter told me Maggie's family are a cold lot,' Flynn stated impassively, 'whereas you're all fire and passion.'

The last word hung in the air although he seemed unaware of it as he walked across and casually refilled his glass, returning a few moments later and settling himself in the chair again, in the same disturbing male pose.

It wasn't ethical for a venerable brain surgeon to be so sexy, surely? Marigold asked herself waspishly. Weren't men in Flynn's position supposed to be past middle age, preferably balding, married, with children and grandchildren? Reassuring father or grandfather fig-ures who were slightly portly and about as sexually at-tractive as a block of wood. She could just imagine the furore he created when he walked on to a ward, espe-cially with the cool, remote and somewhat cynical air he had about him. An air that said he'd seen and done everything and nothing could surprise him. Although she had!

The thought, silly as it was, was immensely gratifying, but after the comment about her expressive face she should have been on her guard, because in the next moment Flynn said, 'OK, let's have it. What's amused you?'

'Amused me?' she prevaricated weakly, hastily wiping all satisfaction from her face. 'I don't know what you mean.'

He shrugged easily. 'Have it your own way. So, who's the guy and is he still in the background somewhere?'

'I didn't say there was a man,' she objected sharply, any lingering smugness gone in an instant.

'Ah, but you didn't say there wasn't, which is more to the point.'

One more 'ah' and she'd throw her glass at his arrogant head, Marigold promised herself, before thinking, Oh, what the heck? She was never going to see him again once she was out of here, so she might as well humour him.

'The man was my fiancé,' she said abruptly, 'and at present he is on what was supposed to be our honeymoon with his new lady friend. OK? Does that satisfy you?'

If nothing else she had surprised him again but somehow it gave her no pleasure this time.

Flynn had sat up in his seat as she had spoken, expelling a quiet breath as he looked at her taut face. 'I'm sorry,' he said very softly, astonishing her with the deep sincerity in his voice, which was smoky warm. 'The guy is a moron but of course you are already aware of that.'

She blinked at him. She'd received various words of

comfort and condolence since she'd thrown Dean's ring at him and sent him packing, but not quite like this.

She relaxed a little, her voice steady as she said, 'Apparently, if one or two mutual friends are to be believed, she probably wasn't the first. We were together for three years and I never suspected a thing.' She gave a mirthless smile. 'What does that make me?'

'Lucky.' It was very dry. 'That you're now rid of him, I mean. You could wait around all your life for him to grow up and die waiting. Let someone else have the job of babysitting him while you have a life instead.'

She'd never heard it put so succinctly before but Marigold realised he was absolutely right. Even when they had still been together, she thought suddenly, she had carried Dean and been the source of strength for them both. She had never been the sort of girl who couldn't say boo to a goose and expected the man in her life to make all the decisions, mind you, but with Dean she had found herself constantly making the decisions for both of them simply because he wouldn't. It had been a flawed relationship in every sense of the word, and the main problem had been—as this stranger had just pointed out—that Dean hadn't grown up. He was still a Jack the lad and not ready for a permanent relationship. Perhaps he never would be; some men were like that.

She raised her head now and looked at Flynn, and the mercurial eyes were waiting for her, their depths as smoky as his voice had been. 'Her name is Tamara, the resident babysitter,' she said with a small smile. 'Apparently she's five feet ten, blonde and blue-eyed, and has legs that go right up to her neck—so I've heard.'

'The mutual friends again?' he asked quietly.

Marigold nodded.

'Seems to me you could do with some new friends, too.'

She'd been thinking along the same lines; hence the increasing urge for a change. She was still too closely linked with Dean in London. They had had the same group of friends for years, went to the same restaurants and pubs, even their places of work were within a mile of each other. As yet she hadn't bumped into him but it was only a matter of time, and this whole thing—Tamara and the broken engagement—had brought about some deep introspection. And as she had examined her mental and emotional processes she'd discovered several things.

One, she could survive quite well in a world in which Dean wasn't the be-all and end-all. Two, there were only a handful of their so-called friends who were what she would *really* term friends. Three, if it wasn't for Dean and their marriage plans she would have spread her wings and gone self-employed ages ago, and probably moved away from the big city now she had enough contacts within the business world to have a healthy shot at working for herself. Four, she needed to do something for *herself* right now, and, whether she succeeded or failed in the world's eyes, the doing would be enough for her. It was time to move on.

Marigold's thoughts had only taken a few moments but when her eyes focused on Flynn again she saw that his gaze had narrowed. 'About to tell me to mind my own business?' he asked mildly, surprising her.

'Not at all.' She hesitated a moment, and then told him exactly what she had been thinking, including the change in her working lifestyle. The whole evening had taken on something of a surreal quality by now; whether this was due to the painkillers making her light-headed or the fact that somehow she'd found herself in this palatial house with this extraordinary man, Marigold wasn't sure. Whatever, she could talk quite frankly and he was a good listener—probably partly due to his line of work, she supposed.

He had folded his arms over his chest and settled himself more comfortably in the chair as he studied her earnest face, and when she had finished he nodded slowly. 'Do it,' he said softly, just as the housekeeper opened the door, holding a pair of metal crutches.

'Here we are,' Bertha said brightly. 'These will do the trick. And dinner's ready, if you'd like to come through to the dining room.'

Marigold found it a bit of a struggle as she made her way out of the drawing room and into a room at the end of the hall. Like the magnificent drawing room, this room was a mix of modern and traditional but done in such a way the overall effect was striking. Pale cream voile curtains hung on antique gold poles. The maple-wood floor complemented the intricately carved table and chairs, which were upholstered in a pale cream and beige, with a splash of vibrant colour here and there in the form of a bowl of scarlet hot-house roses and a magnificent five-foot vase in swirling cinnamon, coral and vermilion hues.

The table was large enough to accommodate ten diners with ease, but two places had been laid close to the roaring fire set in a magnificent fireplace of pale cream marble. Marigold eyed the two places with trepidation as it suddenly dawned on her she would be eating alone with Flynn. 'This really wasn't necessary...'

'I always eat in here when I'm home.' Flynn's voice was just behind her. 'Bertha has merely set another place.'

Did that mean he normally ate alone? Marigold didn't

like to ask outright but it appeared that was what he had meant, and she found it curiously disturbing. This massive house and all the luxury that went with it, and yet he ate alone. But she hadn't for a moment assumed he was married, she realised suddenly. Why was that? She frowned to herself as she carefully sank down onto the chair Flynn had pulled out for her.

'You are allowed just one glass of wine with those pills.' Flynn indicated the bottle of red and the bottle of white wine in front of them. 'Which would you prefer?'

'Red, please.' Marigold answered automatically because her brain had just informed her why she'd sensed Flynn was a bachelor. There was an innate aloofness about him, a cool detachment that spoke of autocratic autonomy, of non-involvement. He would have women, of course, she told herself as she looked into the dark, handsome face. His need for sexual satisfaction was evident in the sensuous mouth and virile body. But he was the sort of man who always kept something back; who gave just enough to keep his lovers satisfied physically but that was all.

And then she caught her errant thoughts self-consciously, telling herself not to be so ridiculous. How on earth did she know anything at all about this man? She had never set eyes on him before today, and she wasn't exactly the greatest authority on men! She had had the odd boyfriend before Dean but they had never got beyond a little fumbling and the odd passionate goodnight kiss, and even with Dean she had insisted they keep full intimacy as something special for their wedding night. She was enormously glad about that with hindsight. Even the degree of intimacy they *had* shared made her flesh creep now when she knew he had been making love to other women whilst they were engaged.

'To chance encounters.' Flynn had filled her glass and then his own, and now he raised the dark red liquid in a toast, a wry smile on his face as he added, 'And mistaken identity.'

It was the first time he had referred to her deception since his initial outburst, and Marigold's cheeks were pink as she responded in like fashion, glad he seemed to be taking things so well.

He turned out to be a charming dinner companion; attentive, amusing, with a dry, slightly wicked sense of humour she wouldn't have suspected at their initial meeting.

Bertha served a rich vegetable soup to start with, which was accompanied by delicious home-made crusty rolls, followed by honey and mustard lamb with celeriac stuffing, and for dessert a perfectly luxurious, smooth and velvety chocolate terrine topped with whipped cream and strawberries. Beans on toast couldn't even begin to compete with Bertha's cooking, Marigold thought dreamily as she licked the last of the chocolate off her spoon.

At the coffee stage her ankle was beginning to hurt again, and she didn't demur when Flynn insisted on her taking another pill—a sleeping tablet this time, he informed her. She was soon more tired than she had ever felt in the whole of her life, the accumulation of the exhausting day, the week or so before when she had worked her socks off to get away a couple of days before Christmas Eve when the roads would be horrendous, and not least the emotional turmoil of the last few months catching up with her in a big way.

Whether it was Flynn's professional eye or the fact that he had had enough of her company for one day, Marigold didn't know, but as she finished the last of the dregs of her coffee-cup he said quietly, 'You need to go straight to bed and sleep for at least nine hours, young lady. Bertha will show you to your room; it's on the ground floor so you haven't got any stairs to negotiate.'

He rose as he spoke and as though by magic Bertha appeared in the next instant. As Flynn helped her to her feet and positioned the crutches under her arms Marigold was terribly aware of his touch in a way that made her jittery and cross with herself. She was a grown woman, for goodness' sake, she told herself irritably as she stitched a bright smile on her face and thanked him for the meal and his hospitality very politely.

'You are welcome,' he said drily, his face unreadable.

She stared at him for a moment, aware she had never really apologised for misleading him about who she was. And it must have made him feel a fool in front of Bertha's husband. Although…somehow she couldn't imagine Flynn Moreau ever feeling a fool. She spoke quickly before she lost her nerve, conscious of Bertha waiting to lead her to her room. 'I…I'm sorry about earlier,' she said quietly, feeling her cheeks beginning to burn. 'I should have explained the situation properly rather than letting you assume I was Emma.'

He smiled the devastating smile she'd seen once before, stopping her breath, before saying lazily, 'I should have known better.'

'Better?' she asked, puzzled.

'Than to let my brain tell my senses that what they were saying was untrue.'

She still didn't understand and her expression spoke for itself.

'The Emma I've heard about is a pert, brash, modern miss with about as much soul as the average Barbie doll,' Flynn said coolly. 'The girl I met on the road didn't tie up with that description at all.'

Marigold stared at him, utterly taken aback by the unexpected compliment. She tried to think of something to say but her brain had put itself on hold, and all she managed was a fairly breathless, 'Thank you.'

'Goodnight, Marigold.' His eyes were unreadable and his voice wasn't particularly warm, but she was conscious of tiny little flickers of sensation racing along every nerve and sinew in a way that was alarming.

'Goodnight.' She began to hobble to the door Bertha was now holding open for her, finding the crutches were a lot more difficult to manipulate than she'd imagined. She turned in the doorway, glancing back at Flynn, who was standing by the fireplace, looking at her. He appeared very dark and still in the dim light from the wall-lights and with the glow from the fire silhouetting his powerful frame. She swallowed hard, not understanding the racing of her pulse as she said, 'I'm sure I'll be all right to go to the cottage tomorrow if you wouldn't mind Wilf driving me there? I don't want to intrude, and you must have plans for Christmas.'

He shrugged easily. 'A few house guests are arriving on Christmas Eve, but one more makes no difference,' he assured her quietly. 'We always bring in the tree and dress it in the afternoon and decorate the house; perhaps you'd like to join in if you're still here then?'

He didn't sound as if he was bothered either way and Marigold said again, her voice firmer, 'I'm sure I'll be fine to go tomorrow, but thank you anyway,' before turning and following Bertha along the hall.

Marigold was conscious of a faint and inexplicable feeling of flatness as Bertha led her to the far end of the house. She would leave tomorrow no matter how her ankle was, she told herself fiercely. She just wanted to get to the cottage and be alone; to read, to rest, to eat and sleep and drink when *she* wanted to.

'Here's your rooms, lovey. You'll see it's more of a little flat,' Bertha said cheerfully as she pushed open a door which had been ajar and stood aside for Marigold to precede her. 'I understand the previous owner had it built on for his old mother, who lived with them for a time before she died, but it's handy for any guests who don't like the stairs. I've lit a fire and— *Oh, you!*'

The change in tone made Marigold jump and nearly lose her control of the crutches, and she raised her head to see Bertha scooping a big tabby cat up in her arms who had been lying on a thick rug in front of a blazing fire in what was clearly a small sitting room.

Bertha continued to scold the cat as she picked it up from in front of the fire and put it outside in the small corridor which led into the main hall of the house.

'My cats wouldn't dream of sneaking in here,' the housekeeper said fussily as she bustled back into the room and put another log on the fire while Marigold sank down onto a comfy chair. 'But that one has an eye for the main chance all right. He's straight upstairs if you don't watch him, looking for an open door so he can lie in comfort on one of the beds.'

Bertha's tone was full of self-righteous disapproval, and Marigold said, a touch bewilderedly, 'Whose cat is he?'

'Oh, he was Maggie's,' Bertha said, 'Emma's grandmother, you know? Mr Moreau heard the animals were all going to be put down so they came here.'

'All of them?' Marigold asked in astonishment, remembering something about chickens and an old cow.

Bertha nodded, bringing her chin down into her neck

as she looked at Marigold. 'All of them. Old Flossie, Maggie's collie dog, is no trouble—she's taken to Wilf and goes everywhere with him—and the chickens and cow are outside in the paddock with the barn for when it snows, but that cat!' She shook her head, making her double chin wobble. 'He takes liberties, he does. Rascal, Maggie called him, and it's Rascal by name and Rascal by nature.'

Bertha continued to bustle about as she opened a door and showed Marigold the attractive double bedroom and *en suite*, a tiny cloakroom containing just a loo and minute corner handbasin and a small but compact kitchen. All the other rooms led directly off the sitting room in a fan layout. It was an extremely comfortable and charming little home in itself and overall was about the size of Marigold's flat in London.

After Bertha had left her, Marigold stood for a moment just glancing around her. This huge house *and* a flat in London! Talk about how the other half lived! But there was clearly a softer side to Flynn, as his taking in Emma's grandmother's waifs and strays had proved.

She tottered into the bedroom, which was beautifully decorated in soft creamy shades of lilac and lemon, and sank down on the broderie-anglaise bed cover.

Did he have a girlfriend? Had he ever been married even? She realised she knew practically nothing about him at all, whereas he had drawn out quite a lot about her during the delicious and leisurely meal. She didn't even know how old he was, and although doing what he did for a living must put him over thirty he had the sort of face and muscled physique that could put him anywhere between his late twenties to early forties.

Marigold suddenly frowned to herself. What on earth was she doing, thinking like this, anyway? Flynn's love life was absolutely no concern of hers. Once she left here tomorrow she would never see him again.

She reminded herself of that several times as she got ready for bed when she found her mind wandering again, but once she had snuggled under the covers all thoughts of Flynn and anything else were gone. She was asleep almost immediately; a deep, dreamless slumber that even her swollen ankle couldn't disturb.

CHAPTER FOUR

THE next day dawned clear and bright, and when Marigold limped to the window and looked out into the crystal-white world beyond she was relieved to see the snow was only three or four inches deep. Nevertheless, the feathery mantle on the trees and bushes beyond the window had turned the small garden—which was obviously the flat's own private domain—into a scene from a Christmas card.

Someone, probably Wilf, had brought her suitcase in from the car the night before and placed it in a corner of the bedroom, but the box she had packed her toiletries and make-up in was still on Myrtle's back seat.

The dressing-table mirror told her she resembled a small, white-faced panda, and she groaned slightly as she looked at her reflection. She had only worn a little mascara and foundation the day before, but a little mascara went a long way when it wasn't removed properly and she had only washed her face with soap and water before climbing into bed.

Her injured ankle was throbbing with enough force to make her grit her teeth as she contemplated hopping into the *en suite*, but just as she rose from the dressing-table stool the door opened and Bertha stood there with a breakfast tray. 'Oh, my, you're up bright and early,' the housekeeper said cheerfully as she walked further into the room. 'I thought you'd sleep till I woke you after that pill Mr Moreau gave you—when I dislocated my knee he gave me one, and I nearly slept round the clock. How is the ankle feeling this morning?'

'Not too bad,' Marigold lied firmly, determined she wouldn't stretch Flynn's hospitality another day.

'That's good. Well, you nip back into bed and eat your breakfast,' Bertha said, for all the world as though Marigold was five years of age instead of twenty-five. 'And when you've eaten there's two more of the pain-killers on the tray. I think Mr Moreau thought you'd need them.'

She certainly did, Marigold thought wryly, once she was back in bed again. Even the light duvet seemed like a ten-ton weight on her foot.

However, a good breakfast, followed by the painkill-ers, and then a somewhat wobbly hot shower helped Marigold's sense of well-being, and to her delight she found a gentle facial cleanser in the bathroom cabinet, which took care of the last of the mascara. After cream-ing her face, again courtesy of the bathroom cabinet, she hobbled into the bedroom and blow-dried her hair, and by the time she had delved into her suitcase and donned fresh underwear, jeans and jumper, she felt a hundred times better than when she had first woken.

At least her face had a little natural colour again, she thought critically as she surveyed herself from head to toe before leaving the room an hour or so later, but there was no way she could manage to wear a shoe, or even one of the socks she had packed, on her bad foot. But it didn't matter. She would manage somehow, she de-termined as she wound the bandage in place.

She found she could manage the crutches much better as she made her way out of the little annexe and into the main hall of the house, but then she nearly went sprawling when Flynn suddenly appeared in the doorway of a room to the right of the drawing room where she was making for.

'Good morning.' He smiled at her, a polite smile, and Marigold forced herself to return it as she grappled for control of her brain, which had decided to scramble itself. She had been unconsciously preparing herself for this moment ever since she had first opened her eyes this morning, but it didn't make it any easier when it was actually happening. He was wearing a black denim shirt and jeans, the shirt open at the neck and the sleeves rolled up to his elbows, revealing muscled arms dusted with soft black hair, and he seemed to fill the doorway with his dark, flagrant masculinity.

He probably didn't mean to be so intimidating, Marigold told herself silently, but there was a magnetic quality to his good looks which drew even as it repelled. His whole persona gave off an air of remoteness and cool detachment, yet there was a seductiveness there that would make any woman worth her salt wonder what it would be like to be made love to by this man.

She killed the last thought stone dead as she replied very formally, 'Good morning. I must thank you again for all your kindness yesterday.'

'Not necessary.' His gaze moved over her steadily as he said, 'How are you feeling?'

'Fine.' She had noticed the smoky quality to his voice yesterday, she remembered, but today it was more obvious. Probably because at this moment in time he wasn't angry with her! 'There's really no need for me to impose upon you any longer,' she said quickly, 'but if Wilf could help me take everything to the cottage that would be an enormous help.'

'I'm sure something can be arranged.'

Marigold was cross to find she felt hot and flustered,

and it didn't help that Flynn, in stark contrast, was the epitome of contained coolness. 'Thank you.' She forced another smile. 'I'll wait for him in my rooms, then, shall I?'

'I know we got off to an unfortunate start yesterday, Marigold, but I don't actually bite, you know.'

'What?' For a moment she wondered if she had heard right. Her eyes shot to his face and she saw there was a disturbing gleam at the backs of his eyes. 'I don't know what you mean.'

'You're like a cat on a hot tin roof as soon as you set eyes on me,' he said coolly, 'and I know for a certainty that the ankle is not at all "fine". In fact it must be giving you hell.'

'Not at all.' It wasn't so bad, in truth, now the pills had dampened down the worst of the pain.

'Even if you were Maggie's granddaughter you would be welcome to stay until you felt better,' Flynn continued, his gaze tight on her flushed face. 'As it is, there is absolutely no need for you to scurry away like a nervous little mouse.'

Marigold stiffened, instantly furious. As an only child she had learnt at an early age to stand up for herself—there were no siblings to run to or to ask for help. Likewise she had realised that if she wanted friends for company after school and in the holidays she had to make them herself. She had never run away from a situation or a person, and had *always* taken the proverbial bull by the horns, and now this…this arrogant, self-opinionated, high-and-mighty stranger had had the cheek to think he could make a sweeping judgement like that!

'Forgive me, Mr Moreau,' she said icily, 'but I thought your qualifications were in the realm of brain surgery, not psychology. That being the case, I'd keep the amateur psychoanalysis to yourself if I were you.'

He hadn't liked the tone of her voice; it was there in the narrowing of his eyes and the hard line of his mouth, but his voice was soft when he said, 'So you are not afraid of me?'

'I'm not afraid of anyone!'

'This is very good.' There was the slightest of accents to his voice at times, or perhaps not even an accent but a certain way of putting things that made his mixed and somewhat volatile parentage very obvious. 'Then perhaps you would like to have coffee with me?' he suggested silkily. 'Bertha always brings me a tray at about this time.'

She stared at him warily. She couldn't think of anything she would like less but she couldn't very well say so, and so she nodded stiffly, still very much on the defensive as he stood aside for her to enter the room.

It was clearly his study. Books lined two of the walls and a third was taken up by a huge full-length window, which opened out on to a rolling lawn. A fire was burning in a black marble fireplace, and in front of it— stretched out comfortably on a thick rug as though it was a place he was very familiar with—was the big tabby cat. Flynn gestured to a large, plump leather chair in front of the big mahogany desk strewn with papers. 'Make yourself comfortable.'

Comfortable was not an option around this man, Marigold thought ruefully as she duly seated herself, expecting Flynn to take the massive chair behind the desk, where he had clearly been working. Instead he stood looking down at her for a moment, his eyes wandering over the clear oval face and creamy skin and lingering on the delicate bone-structure, before he perched himself easily on the edge of the desk in front of her.

'I would like you to spend Christmas here,' he said coolly without any lead-up at all. 'OK?'

Not OK. Definitely, definitely *not* OK. Rascal was now purring as he rolled on his back for a moment in the warmth from the fire, fanning the air with plump paws for a moment or two before he sank back into contented immobility.

Flynn probably viewed her like Emma's grandmother's waifs and strays, Marigold thought ignominiously, especially after she had revealed her reason for deciding to spend Christmas at the cottage all alone. Why, oh, why had she told him about Dean? Did he think she was playing for the sympathy vote? She steeled her humiliation not to come through in her voice as she said politely, 'I really couldn't do that. You've said you already have guests coming to stay.'

'I also said that one more won't make any difference,' he reminded her smoothly.

'Nevertheless…'

'You're not fit enough to be in that cottage alone and you know it,' he challenged quietly.

She'd been right. He *did* view her as poor little orphan Annie. 'I disagree.' She smiled brightly. 'I've food, warmth—and I intend to just veg out for a few days. Emma's coming at some point anyway.' She wished he'd move off the desk and into his chair; somehow he seemed twice as intimidating than usual in his present position, and she was uncomfortably aware of hard, powerful male thighs just a few inches away from her face.

'So I can't persuade you?' the deep, dark voice asked silkily.

'No, you can't.'

It was so definite the dark brows rose slowly in disparaging amusement. 'Pity.'

Bertha tapped on the door at that moment and then entered with a steaming tray holding a coffee-pot, cup and saucer and a plate of what looked like home-made shortcake. 'Another cup and saucer, please, Bertha, and milk and sugar. You do take milk and sugar?' he asked Marigold, who nodded quickly, and then felt herself deflate with relief when he slid off the desk and walked round to his chair as Bertha disappeared.

She searched her mind for something reasonably impersonal to say. 'So you've lived here for a couple of years?' she said carefully. 'Isn't it a little remote and far from London?'

He shrugged powerful shoulders and for a moment her senses went into hyperdrive before she got them under control again. 'That's what made it so attractive when Peter decided to sell. I had a place in London at the time and although it was very comfortable in its own grounds—' she could imagine, Marigold thought waspishly '—I was always on top of the job, so to speak. I'd been looking for somewhere like this for some time but the right location hadn't presented itself. Peter and I did the deal in weeks, which suited his circumstances, and after buying the flat in London I moved most of the furniture here. The only stipulation from Peter was that I'd keep an eye on Maggie for him; he was very fond of the old lady and within a few minutes of meeting her I could understand why.'

'I'm sure Emma's family didn't mean to be neglectful—' Marigold began, only to be interrupted by an abrupt wave of his hand.

'Spare me any platitudes.'

She glared at him. He was the rudest man she had ever met by far! She had heard it said that medical consultants and such considered themselves one step down from the Almighty, and now she was beginning to believe it.

Bertha returned with the other cup and saucer before Marigold could think of an adequately scathing retort, and while they drank the coffee and ate the shortbread Flynn kept the conversation pleasant and easy. Marigold had briefly considered sulking, but in view of the fact that he had opened up his home to her she decided a few more minutes of tolerance weren't completely beyond her.

As soon as she'd finished, however, she launched herself a little awkwardly to her feet. 'I'll be off, then,' she said quietly as Flynn rose in his turn. 'Thank you very much indeed for all you've done.'

'Flynn.'

'What?' He'd said his name very softly.

'The name is Flynn,' he persisted irascibly. 'You've avoided calling me anything at all rather than say my name, haven't you?'

She'd call him lots of things if only he did but know it. 'Not at all,' she lied quickly, knowing he was absolutely right. Somehow calling him Flynn took this situation to another dimension, and once she'd said it if they met again in the future—heaven forbid—she couldn't very well go back to Mr Moreau. And she needed to keep a distance between herself and this man; emotionally and mentally as well as physically. She didn't dwell on the thought; she didn't dare, not with Flynn right in front of her. She would examine it later when she was alone.

'Not at all,' he repeated with velvety sarcasm. 'That's

twice you've said those words this morning and each time you've been lying through your pretty white teeth.'

'How dare you?' Marigold stared at him, her face flushed with guilty annoyance. 'You've got no right to talk to me like that.'

'Rights are something to be taken, not given,' he said with silky emphasis. 'Did you call the tune with your fiancé all the time? Train him to walk to heel, that sort of thing?'

'I don't believe I'm hearing this—'

'Because it wouldn't do with a real man, my sweet little warrior,' he drawled coolly, his tone in direct contrast to her outraged voice.

'And you're a real man, are you?' she shot back with furious indignation.

'Oh, yes.' He had walked round the other side of the desk to stand just in front of her, the crystal eyes vivid in the dark tanned face and his mouth twisted in a sardonic smile as he viewed her shocked rage. 'And a real man is what you need, Marigold. Fire needs to be met with fire if it isn't to gradually die and turn to ashes or, worse still, burn up itself and everything around it. For every woman who's an out-and-out shrew there's a weak man somewhere in the background.'

For the first time in Marigold's life she was so furious that words failed her. Her eyes shooting blue sparks and her cheeks burning with angry, violent colour, she silently railed at the need to hold on to the crutches. She would have given everything she owned in that moment to be able to smack him hard across his arrogant, self-satisfied face, big as he was. However, there was absolutely no way she was going to risk falling flat on her face for the privilege!

She turned in one angry, sweeping movement and

made for the door, but Flynn was there before her, opening it with a flourish as he said calmly, 'I'll get Wilf to bring your things down, shall I?'

'Thank you!' It was a bark, which made his lips twitch. Marigold saw the amusement he couldn't hide and willed herself to ignore it, pattering down the hall as fast as she could and into the little corridor leading to her rooms. She opened the door to the sitting room with trembling fingers, so upset she didn't know if she wanted to cry or scream and nearly losing her balance in the process.

In the event she neither screamed nor cried, but sat waiting for Wilf with a straight back and a burning face once she had closed the suitcase and slipped on her thick fleece. Impossible man! Utterly, utterly impossible man! And she hadn't asked him for help in the first place. Well, reason interrupted, she *had* hoped for a lift to Emma's cottage when she'd flagged him down on the road, but that was all. She hadn't asked to come here. She hadn't asked to spend the night. And she definitely hadn't asked for his opinion on her, or her life.

It was a further ten minutes before Wilf knocked on the outer door, and by then Marigold was calmer, at least outwardly. Inwardly she still wanted to kick something—or someone to be exact. That someone was waiting in the hall when she followed Wilf into the main house, and as the other man continued outside with the suitcase Marigold said very stiffly to Flynn, 'Would you thank Bertha for me for all her kindness?'

'Certainly.' He reached for a leather jacket on a chair near by and pulled open the front door—which had swung partially closed—to enable her to pass through.

'And I'll get Emma to pop the crutches back when

she arrives,' Marigold added tightly, hating the fact that he was coming outside to watch her depart.

Only he wasn't.

The massive 4x4 was parked on the drive with the suitcase on the back seats, but Wilf was nowhere to be seen. Marigold reached the vehicle with Flynn just behind her, and as he said, 'Here, let me help you,' she found herself lifted into the passenger seat before she could utter any protest. He then proceeded to walk round the bonnet and climb into the driver's seat, as cool as a cucumber.

'What are you doing?' She knew her voice was too shrill but she couldn't help it.

'I thought you wanted to go to the cottage? Have you changed your mind?' he asked helpfully.

'No, I have not changed my mind,' Marigold snapped testily. 'I thought Wilf was taking me.'

'I don't know who told you that. As far as I recall, I said nothing beyond Wilf would bring your case to the car.'

'But I told you—'

'Ah, but I won't be told, Marigold, as I thought we'd already ascertained,' Flynn said with unforgivable satisfaction. 'I wouldn't dream of delegating the responsibility of seeing one of my guests to her new accommodation to Wilf, not when I'm available,' he added as the powerful engine kicked into life. 'Wilf will drive your car over at some point in the next couple of days but, as you can't possibly drive with that foot, there is no hurry, is there?'

It was so reasonable that Marigold felt like a recalcitrant child, which no doubt was *exactly* how Flynn wanted her to feel, she thought irritably.

The 4x4 ate up the short distance across the valley to

the cottage before Marigold could blink, or at least that was what it felt like. She wouldn't have admitted to a living soul that her spirit shrank at having to enter the damp, dark little house again, but the pale winter sunshine did light up the outside of the cottage beautifully, she thought as Flynn parked at the small gate and then walked round the car to help her descend.

She steeled herself for the rush of damp air and chilliness as Flynn opened the front door with the key she had given him the day before so Wilf could get some heat into the cottage, but instead of the dank, dismal air she remembered the tiny hall was warm and welcoming.

He opened the door to the sitting room for her, and the fusty, damp room of yesterday had been transformed into a still undeniably crowded but bright, warm and charming room. A crackling fire was burning in the grate, two bowls of sweetly perfumed, colourful flowers added a real homely touch, and, with the drapes at the windows pulled back to disclose the white wonderland outside, the cottage couldn't have been more different from her memory.

'We've kept the heaters on night and day so I'm afraid the electricity might be a bit heavy,' Flynn said quietly at her side. 'But it was necessary. Wilf took them away today; now it's warmed through the fires in here and the bedroom will be enough to keep it up to temperature.'

'It's lovely.' She couldn't believe how a bright log fire and bowls of flowers could bring such enchantment to a place, but they had. Everything seemed different. She was suddenly seeing the cottage through the eyes of Emma's grandmother, and her heart went out to the old lady who had fought so hard to remain in her home.

She limped through to the bedroom, where another glowing fire met her, along with fresh sheets and an exquisite broderie-anglaise bed cover in cream linen. Marigold recognised the design. 'This is one of your bedspreads from the house, isn't it?' she said slowly, her eyes taking in more flowers on the dressing table and chest of drawers.

Flynn gave the nonchalant shrug she was beginning to recognise. 'Spares, apparently, which Bertha had in one of her cupboards,' he said dismissively.

'And the flowers?'

'Wilf has a couple of greenhouses in the grounds. He keeps Bertha supplied with flowers for the house and there are always more than we can use.'

Marigold wasn't fooled by the casual words. Flynn had organised all this and she was grateful, she really was, but she was frightened of how pleased she felt. He'd do the same for any foundling he discovered lost in the storm, she reminded herself with wry, caustic humour; this didn't mean anything. And that was fine, just fine, because she didn't *want* it to mean anything. She had just come out of one disastrous relationship—she didn't need anymore emotional turmoil.

'It's so different.' He was right behind her, standing in the bedroom doorway as she turned, and when he didn't move she said quickly, 'You shouldn't have gone to so much trouble but I do appreciate it. What do I owe you for the fuel?'

'Don't be so ridiculous,' he said softly.

Marigold could feel her heart racing, a frantic, fast thud that made her unable to think coherently. She stared up at him, vitally aware of the broad male bulk of him and of her own fragility. 'But I must pay you,' she insisted faintly. 'I couldn't possibly—'

His head lowered as his hands gently gripped her upper arms and the kiss was everything she knew it would be. It was gentle and exploring at first, his mouth caressing and warm and firm, and when she made no effort to push him away it deepened subtly into a sensual invasion that had her making small female sounds of pleasure low in her throat.

'Your hair feels like spun silk,' he murmured against her soft lips, one hand entangled in the chestnut veil as he pulled her head back to allow himself greater access to her mouth. 'And the colours in it are enchanting. I've never seen anyone with such beautiful hair; do you know that?'

Marigold didn't answer him; she *couldn't* answer him. She was dazed and shaking, utterly bewildered by the desire he had aroused with just a kiss. A *kiss*. She had never felt like this once in all her time with Dean.

He took her mouth again, biting gently and expertly at her bottom lip in between kissing her with increasing passion. He had drawn her onto the hardness of his male frame now, their bodies so close she could feel what the kiss was doing for him. One hand was warm and firm against the small of her back and the other was stroking her face, throat and shoulder, soft, sensuous, light caresses that were sending her nerve-endings into quivering delight.

He was so *good* at this; his mouth first languorous and then fierce, teasing and then demanding as it moved against hers with complete mastery. He was ravaging her inner sweetness now and dimly Marigold realised she was kissing him right back, just as passionately.

His fingers brushed against one full breast and then the other before exploring the slender width of her tiny waist, and then, with a low sound of protest deep in his throat, his mouth lifted from hers and he eased her away from him very slowly, still taking care to hold her upright.

'You see?' he said very softly. 'Fire with fire.'

Marigold stared at him, her eyes slowly losing their dazed, fluid expression as reality dawned in all its chilling horror now he wasn't kissing her any more. This man was someone she didn't like; they had barely said more than two civil words to each other since they'd first met, and she had allowed him... She didn't like to think what she had allowed.

He must have sensed something of what she was feeling because his voice was dry when he spoke again, carrying the hidden amusement she'd heard several times before as he said, 'It's all right, Marigold. It was just a kiss.'

No, it wasn't just a kiss, she thought with blinding humiliation, at least not to her. It was easily the most mind-blowing experience of her life and had taught her more about herself in a few moments than in the last twenty-five years; the most important thing being—she didn't have a clue who she really was. If anyone had told her she could lose her head like this she would have laughed in their face, but it had happened. It had happened. And it mustn't happen again.

'Please let go of me.' Her voice was small but clear, and he complied immediately.

What must he be thinking? Marigold asked herself with silent desperation. One day she was telling him how she'd come to Emma's cottage to nurse a broken heart— the next she'd practically eaten him alive! She made no apology for exaggerating on both counts.

'I'm not going to say I'm sorry for kissing you because I wanted to do so even from that first moment on the road,' Flynn said with careful flatness. 'Neither will I pretend not to notice that you enjoyed it.'

She didn't deny this—there would have been no point and Marigold had never been one for dodging the consequences of her actions. Instead she raised her small chin and slanted her eyes—her body language speaking volumes to the tall, dark man watching her so closely—and said tightly, 'I would like you to leave now but first I must pay you for the logs and coal.'

'It was a kiss, for crying out loud!' Flynn rasped irritably, raking a hand through his dark hair in a manner that spoke of extreme frustration. 'Between two consenting adults, I might add. Now, if we had ended up in bed I might be able to understand you feeling slightly…manoeuvred.'

'There was absolutely no question of that,' Marigold snapped angrily. He'd be telling her she was anybody's next! 'I barely know you.'

Dark eyebrows rose mockingly as he crossed powerful arms over his chest. 'Flynn Moreau, thirty-eight, single, and of sound mind,' he offered lazily. 'Anything else you'd deem important?'

'Plenty.'

'Then we'll have to see to that in due course,' he said very softly, and suddenly he wasn't smiling.

'I don't think so.' She tried very hard to make her voice sound firm in spite of the fact her stomach had turned to jelly. He was *interested* in her? She couldn't quite believe it. Men like him—successful, wealthy, charismatic and powerful—went for the tall, leggy blonde model types; Tamara types. Worldly women who knew all the right gossip and wore the right clothes, and who had a list of friends that ran like the current *Who's Who*. She was five-feet-four with straight chestnut-brown hair and a skin that sprouted freckles in the summer, and even her mother couldn't call her a ravishing beauty. Perhaps he thought a little dalliance over the holiday period might be entertaining? Especially as she was on the doorstep, so to speak.

'No?' His voice held the softest edge of irony and he didn't seem at all put out at her refusal to play ball. It confirmed her theory more than anything else could have done. 'Still pining after what might have been?'

For a moment she didn't understand to what he was referring, and then she remembered Dean. Dean. Who hadn't stirred her senses or aroused her body remotely when compared to this man, and who now seemed a very distant memory indeed. Which was frightening, scary, when taking into account that but for Tamara she would now be Mrs Dean Barker. 'Not at...' She stopped abruptly when the silver eyes glittered a challenge. 'No, I am not pining for what might have been,' she said instead, very slowly and very firmly. 'In fact, for some time now I've felt I had a lucky escape.' The time in question being since Flynn had kissed her and she'd known, for the first time, what it was like to actually meet a man passion for passion. She would never have felt like that about Dean, not in a million years.

'But he's shaken your trust in the male of the species,' Flynn said intuitively. 'Hasn't he?'

Yes, he had, and it was annoying that she hadn't realised that till now either, Marigold thought irritably. Mr He-Who-Knows-All-Things here would just love it if she admitted that little golden nugget. 'I'm sorry if that's the only way you can accept that I don't want to get to know you any further,' she said primly.

'So I'm not right?'

She took a deep hidden breath and lied through the pretty white teeth again. 'No, you are not.'

He smiled; a predatory, shark-like smile if she thought about it, Marigold noticed uneasily. 'I'm pleased you're not an accomplished liar, Marigold,' he said charmingly. 'I really don't like that in a woman. Now, there is a small lean-to and hut just outside the kitchen door; Maggie used to keep the chickens in there when the weather was bad. Wilf's stocked it with logs and coal— more than enough for a couple of weeks' fuel—and you must keep the fires going day and night. You know how to bank a fire, I suppose?'

She didn't have a clue, but she nodded stiffly. 'Of course I do,' she said haughtily.

He eyed her mockingly. 'Plenty of damp slack does the trick, along with tea leaves or vegetable peelings; that sort of thing. Pile it on thick just before you turn in and make sure as little air as possible is getting to the fire. That way you should still have enough glowing embers to get it going nicely in the morning once you've scooped the ash into a bucket.'

Quite the little downstairs maid, wasn't he? Marigold thought nastily, and then felt immediately ashamed of herself when Flynn added, 'Your groceries are all packed away in the cupboards and the fridge is stocked. There's no freezer, I'm afraid.'

'Right, thank you. Now, what do I—?'

'If you mention payment once more I'll take it,' Flynn warned with a glint in his eye, 'but it won't be of the financial kind. Do you understand?'

She opened her mouth to protest, looked into his eyes and knew he meant it. Her mouth closed again. She was just eternally grateful he'd never know the way his words had made her flesh tingle and the blood sing through her veins.

'Take these every six hours; no more than eight in twenty-four hours,' he warned quietly, suddenly very much the professional as he brought a small bottle of the painkillers out of his pocket. 'And no more than the odd glass of wine whilst you're taking them.'

She nodded, wishing he'd just go. She needed time to sort out her whirling thoughts and utter confusion, and whilst he was here in front of her there was no chance of her racing emotions being brought under control.

He stepped closer again, lifting a hand to cup her chin as he said, 'Goodbye, Marigold.'

'Goodbye.' Suddenly, and with an irrationality that surprised her, she wanted to beg him to stay. Which was crazy, she warned herself, wondering if he was going to kiss her again.

He didn't.

What was wrong with her? Marigold asked herself crossly as she watched Flynn turn and walk to the door. She couldn't be attracted to him; she wouldn't let herself be. Her life was difficult enough at the moment and she had some major changes in view for the new year and the last thing she needed was a complication like Flynn!

She followed him to the front door and watched the tall, dark figure stride across the snow where the path should have been. The blue sky above him was piercingly clear, and a white winter sun had turned the snow into a mass of glittering diamonds in which the indentation of his large footsteps stood out with stark severity. They were like him—utterly larger than life.

Marigold narrowed her eyes against the sunlight as her thoughts sped on. Flynn was one of those characters you came across just a few times in a lifetime; the sort of person who created atmosphere and life wherever they went, sweeping lesser mortals into their orbit for a short time until they moved on to pastures new. It would be fatal to get involved in any way with a man like that.

He had talked about meeting fire with fire, but he didn't know her, not really. She was just ordinary—she wanted a home and family eventually, with the right man. Most of all she wanted someone who loved her, who was completely hers. Someone who thought she was wonderful just as she was and who would never look at a tall, beautiful blonde with legs that went right up to her armpits.

She watched the 4x4 move away, lifting her hand briefly in acknowledgement of Flynn's wave, and it wasn't until she hobbled back into the cottage and made her way into the kitchen, intending to make a reviving cup of coffee, that she even realised she was crying.

CHAPTER FIVE

WITH a determination Marigold didn't know she was capable of, she put all thoughts of Flynn Moreau out of her mind for the rest of the day and evening. Admittedly he did have an annoying habit of invading her mind if she let her guard down even for a second, but, with the radio kept on pretty loudly and a book in front of her nose which she'd been promising herself she'd read for ages, she managed fairly well.

Once Flynn had gone she'd hobbled out to the kitchen and found the cupboards and fridge stocked with masses of stuff she hadn't bought, along with several little luxuries that brought her eyes opening wide. Several bottles of a particular red wine that she knew cost the earth; an enormous box of chocolates; a mouth-watering dessert that was all meringue and whipped cream and fresh strawberries and raspberries, and which would easily have served eight people... The list went on.

Marigold viewed it all with a mixture of disquiet and pleasure, and when she poked her head out of the back door she saw there were enough logs and coal for two months, let alone two weeks. You couldn't fault him on generosity. She bit on her lip hard as, the clock on the mantelpiece chiming eleven o'clock, she found her thoughts had returned to Flynn once more.

She had allowed herself one glass of the wonderful wine with her evening meal—a succulent steak grilled with mushrooms and tomatoes—and the taste of it was still on her tongue as she rose to prepare for bed. It was as different from the cheap wine she normally indulged in as chalk from cheese, and accentuated the difference in their ways of life more distinctly than anything else so far. He must have a cellar stocked with expensive wine, she thought dismally as she climbed into bed a few minutes later—a bed with crisp, scented sheets and the beautiful broderie-anglaise cover. From her brief glance in the bedroom the day before she remembered the bed had been piled with old, unattractive blankets and what had appeared to be a moth-eaten eiderdown in faded pink satin.

She had followed Flynn's advice and banked down the fires as he'd instructed, and now the tiny blue and orange flames licking carefully round the base of the damp slack caused the shadows in the room to dance slightly, the odd crackle and spit from the fire immensely comforting. It was gorgeous having a real fire to look at whilst you were all cuddled up and snug in bed, Marigold thought sleepily. She could understand why Emma's grandmother had fought to stay here for so long. With a certain amount of elbow grease to get things looking spick and span, a few tins of paint and a clearing out of some of the more dilapidated items of furniture, to give more space and to show off some of what Marigold recognised were really very nice pieces in the sitting room, the cottage could be transformed.

This bedroom was really very large, although packed as it was it didn't seem so. With just the bed and perhaps a new, smaller wardrobe there would be heaps of room for a good working area by the window. She'd easily fit a chair and drawing board and everything else in…

Marigold stopped abruptly, sitting up in bed and flicking back her curtain of hair as she realised where her musing had led. Was she still seriously considering making an offer to Emma for her grandmother's old home? What about all the inconveniences? What about the isolation? *What about Flynn Moreau?*

She sat for some minutes, staring into space, before sliding down into the warm cocoon again. No, it was an impossible idea. Even if she forgot about all the practical difficulties there was still Flynn. Her heart began to pound with reckless speed at the thought of Flynn as her nearest neighbour, and she spoke to it sternly, telling it to behave.

She wasn't going to think about this any more tonight. She turned over onto her side, adjusting her legs so that her good foot protected her aching ankle, and shut her eyes determinedly. It was Christmas Eve tomorrow, she was in a snug little cottage with snow all around her and masses of food and drink, and it was nice to be on her own for once. It *was*. She'd enjoy her Christmas—quietly perhaps, but she'd still enjoy it—and she wasn't going to think about anything more challenging than when the next glass of wine or meal was due. She probably wouldn't even see Flynn Moreau again anyway...

She was asleep within minutes, and it didn't occur to her, as she drifted away into a deep, dreamless slumber, that she hadn't given a single thought to Dean and Tamara for hours.

It was about ten o'clock the next morning when the sound of someone banging on the front door of the cottage brought Marigold jerking awake. For a moment or two she didn't know where she was and then, as it all flooded back, she pushed the covers aside and reached for the new thick, fleecy white robe she had treated herself to as an early Christmas present. It was the sort of thing she'd seen some of the stars of the silver screen wear in fashionable magazines, and although it had cost an arm and a leg it made her feel wonderfully feminine and expensive. And since Tamara she'd needed to feel feminine.

She tested her weight gingerly on her poorly foot and when it felt bearable she limped carefully to the door without bothering to use the crutches, wondering if Wilf was outside with Myrtle. She brushed her cloud of hair from her eyes and opened the door.

'Good morning.'

It was snowing again, she thought dazedly as she stared into a pair of crystal eyes above which jet-black hair was coated with a feathery covering of white, before forcing herself to answer, 'Good morning.'

'I got you out of bed.' He didn't sound at all sorry; in fact his eyes were inspecting her with a relish that made Marigold feel positively undressed rather than wrapped round in an armour of fluffy white towelling.

'Yes,' she agreed vaguely, wondering how any one man had the right to look so sexy when she hadn't even brushed her teeth. 'I didn't bother to set my alarm.'

'I've brought you something.' He indicated with his hand at the side of him and she looked down to see a cute little Christmas tree sitting on the step. 'We've just brought in the one for the house and this was close by and it seemed the right size for the cottage. Bertha's sorted out a few decorations and what have you. It's in a tub and you'll need to keep it damp so it can go back outside after Christmas.'

'Right.' She knew she wasn't sounding very grateful but she was acutely conscious of her tousled hair and make-up-free face.

'How's the foot?'

'The foot?' Marigold made an effort to pull herself

together. 'Oh, the foot. It seems a bit better, thank you,' she managed fairly coherently.

'Good.' He paused, looking down at her with glittering eyes. 'There's not any coffee going, is there?'

Marigold flushed. After his open-handed generosity she could hardly refuse him a cup of coffee, but he looked so immaculately groomed, with every hair in place, and she... Well, she wasn't, she reflected hotly. Although he had nicked himself shaving. Her eyes focused on a tiny cut on the square male chin and she found herself suddenly short of breath.

'Marigold?'

'What?' She blinked, realising he had said something else and she hadn't heard a word.

'I said, if it's too much trouble...'

Marigold's flush deepened. 'Of course not,' she said crossly, and then moderated her tone as she added, 'Please come in, and you can put the tree in the sitting room by the fireplace if you don't mind. It...it's very nice.'

'Yes, it is, isn't it?' he agreed meekly, but she had glanced into the silver eyes again and they were laughing at her.

Once in the sitting room, Flynn looked somewhat accusingly at the faint glow from the embers of the fire. 'It's nearly out. You see to the coffee and I'll see to the fire,' he offered, shrugging off his leather jacket and slinging it onto the sofa as he spoke. 'Have you come across the old bucket Maggie used for the hot ashes?'

'It's in the broom cupboard; I'll get it,' Marigold said hastily. She'd discovered the broom cupboard in an alcove in the kitchen the day before. 'You wait here.' The kitchen was old-fashioned and with barely enough room to swing a cat; the thought of herself and Flynn enclosed in such a small space was daunting to say the least.

She hobbled her way into the kitchen and opened the cupboard door, grabbing the bucket and swinging round, and then she gave a surprised squeak to find Flynn right behind her.

'You shouldn't be walking on that ankle yet; where are the crutches?'

He was wearing a pair of faded blue jeans and a big Aran jumper which was clearly an old favourite today; he'd obviously dressed down for the expedition in the snow to bring in the Christmas trees. The clothes were clean but faintly shabby if anything, and didn't have the designer cut and flair of the others she had seen him in. So why, Marigold asked herself weakly, did they enhance his dark masculinity even more than the others had done?

She forced herself to concentrate on what she was saying as she replied, 'The crutches are by the bed, I suppose, but I'd rather manage without them if I can. The narrow doorways here are not conducive to an extra pair of legs.'

'Nor anyone above the height of five feet six,' Flynn agreed easily. 'It took me a few visits to see Maggie before I learnt to duck.'

Marigold swallowed and tried a smile. His body was so close it was forcing her to acknowledge her awareness of his male warmth, and the faint scent emanating from the tanned skin—a subtle, spicy fragrance—was causing a reaction in her lower stomach she could well have done without. The trouble was, Flynn was such a *disturbing* man that just being around him was enough to make her all fingers and thumbs, Marigold admitted to herself crossly. Even when he was just being friendly and help-ful, like now.

She held up the bucket, unconsciously using it as a defence against his nearness. 'I'll…I'll put the kettle on,' she said a little breathlessly. 'There's only instant coffee, I'm afraid; Maggie clearly didn't run to a coffee maker.'

'No, Maggie was the proverbial cup of tea and hot buttered scones type.' A black eyebrow quirked. 'There *are* some croissants in the bread bin, though, along with one of Bertha's home-made loaves, if you're offering?'

She hadn't been aware she was. She didn't answer immediately. 'Breakfast seems like years ago when you've been working in the fresh air for a while,' he murmured with blatant scheming.

'Oh, I'm sorry; I thought you'd brought in a couple of Christmas trees,' Marigold said severely, 'not a whole forest.'

He grinned at her, utterly unrepentant at his persis-tence, and Marigold floundered. 'Croissants it is, then,' she agreed quickly, just wishing he would move and put a little more space between them. 'And I suppose you know where the preserves are, too?'

'Left-hand cupboard above the sink,' Flynn answered meekly. 'And I prefer blackcurrant.'

'You'll get what you're given.'

'Promises, promises…'

But he had taken the bucket and was walking out of the kitchen and she could breathe again.

'And don't try to carry a tray or anything,' he called over his shoulder. 'I'll come and see to it once the fire's blazing.'

By half-past ten Marigold was seated in front of a roaring fire which contrasted beautifully with the swirl-ing snowflakes outside the sitting-room window, eating croissants warmed in the kitchen's big old oven. Flynn demolished five to her two—his liberally covered with blackcurrant preserve—after which he said pensively, 'Ever tried toast made over an open fire?'

'You can't still be hungry!'

'I burn off a lot of energy.' He eyed her over his coffee mug and she didn't ask how.

They found a toasting fork among the instruments hanging on a black iron stand on the hearth, and once Flynn had cut the bread and begun toasting it over the fire the smell was so wonderful that Marigold found herself eating a piece dripping with melting butter even though she was full up.

This was too cosy by half. She slanted a glance at Flynn under her eyelashes. He was busy toasting his second doorstep, crouched down in front of the fire in a manner which stretched the denim tight over lean, strong hips and muscled thighs. He had a magnificent body... The thought came from nowhere and shocked her into choking on an errant crumb.

How on earth had she come to be sitting here in her dressing gown, sharing breakfast with a man she had only known for a couple of days? Marigold asked herself faintly. But she knew the answer—because the man in question went by the name of Flynn Moreau. He was like a human bulldozer, she thought with a touch of desperate bewilderment—riding roughshod over any objections or difficulties in his path to get what he wanted.

Did he want her? She risked another glance and then stiffened as she met his eyes. 'What's the matter?' he asked softly.

'The matter?'

'You were frowning.'

'Was I?' she prevaricated feebly. She managed to divert him by making some excuse about twinges in her foot, before she quickly moved on to the fact she needed a hot bath and to get dressed.

'Go ahead,' he offered blandly. 'I'll wash up and then set up the Christmas tree.'

'No, it's all right really.' The thought of Flynn in the cottage while she lay naked in the bath was unthinkable. 'You must have lots to do back at the house, and didn't you say you had guests arriving today?'

'Later,' he agreed smoothly.

'Well, I'd like to have a really long, hot soak,' she persisted firmly, 'and I shan't feel comfortable doing that if I know I'm keeping you waiting. It…it'll be good for my ankle,' she added.

He stared at her but the doctor in him won. 'OK.' He stood up in one lithe, graceful male movement and she blinked. 'I don't suppose it's any good my offering to wash your back?' he suggested softly.

'No good at all.'

'Shame.'

Yes, it was rather. Marigold smiled brightly. 'Thank you very much for the Christmas tree, and thank Bertha for the decorations for me, would you?' she said evenly.

'You can thank her yourself later,' Flynn returned just as evenly as he walked to the door.

'I'm sorry?'

'Oh, didn't I mention it?' He opened the sitting-room door, passing through to the hall, and she heard his voice in the moments before he shut the door after him say coolly, 'I'm picking you up at six tonight for the party at my house.'

Marigold wouldn't have believed she could move so quickly but she was at the front door within moments, yanking it open and calling to the dark figure making his way to the 4x4 parked at the end of the garden. 'Flynn? *Flynn!*'

'You bellowed, ma'am?' He turned, shrugging on the leather jacket as he did so, and she tried to ignore how good he looked as she said, 'I can't possibly come to your party; you know I can't.'

'I know nothing of the sort,' he returned mildly.

'I can hardly walk, for one thing.'

'You said your ankle was a little better.'

'Not better enough for a party,' Marigold objected.

'You don't have to dance if you don't want to.'

They were having dancing. Dancing meant dance dresses. 'I can't possibly come,' she said again, her voice even firmer. 'I've absolutely nothing to wear. I came here just to crash out for a few days if you remember, and anyway, I was looking forward to a quiet Christmas Eve at the cottage in front of the fire.'

He tilted his head. 'You're twenty-five, right?'

Marigold nodded warily, big, fat, starry flakes of snow drifting idly onto the hall mat.

'Beautiful twenty-five-year-olds don't look forward to sitting all alone in front of a fire like old women on Christmas Eve,' Flynn stated silkily, but she'd caught the metallic chink of steel under the velvety softness of his tone.

She felt the 'beautiful' melting her resistance and fought the weakness with all her might. 'This one does,' she said flatly.

'You're coming, Marigold. As to the clothes, you needn't worry. The bunch who are coming tonight could be dressed in anything from jeans to Dior.' He had walked back to the cottage door as he'd been speaking and now he reached out for her, his firm, slightly stern and very sensuous mouth smiling.

What were the odds on it being the Dior, Marigold asked herself wryly, but with his fingertips against her lower ribs, and the warmth of his palms cupping her sides sending pulsing sensation through her body, it was hard to concentrate on anything but his closeness.

Nevertheless, she opened her mouth to object but before she could say a word his lips had snatched it away, plunging swiftly into the undefended territory as he took full advantage of her momentary uncertainty. This time there was no gentle persuasion; the kiss was hot and potent and dangerous, feeding a heady rush of wild sensation that had her gasping against his mouth. He pulled her hard into him until she felt she was branded against his maleness; the sensation more intimate than all the caresses she had shared with Dean.

This was what it should be like, she thought headily as her senses swam. This need, this desire, this overwhelming, driving urge to get closer and closer. For the first time in her life she was revelling in the knowledge that she was a woman, one half of a perfect whole.

She could feel his heart pounding like a sledgehammer against the solid wall of his chest, and then, as his hands moved beneath the thick towelling and found the warm, soft silk of her nightie, the flesh beneath firm and taut, she trembled helplessly.

She felt this man was an alien being, a dark, powerful stranger who could sweep her into another world without even trying, and yet at the same time she felt she had known him since the world began, that he had always been part of her. She shivered, the extent of her need frightening, and immediately she felt him move away. 'You're cold.' His voice was rueful, and she hated him that he could even formulate words when she was feeling so utterly devastated. 'Go and have that hot bath and I'll see you tonight.'

She didn't say anything for the simple reason she couldn't, but after he had left, in a swirl of snow as he drove the big vehicle hard towards the house on the other side of the valley, she berated herself a hundred times as she lay soaking in the warm, bubbly water.

She must be mad, stark, staring mad, to agree to go to this party tonight! Not that she had actually agreed, she comforted herself vainly, not in so many words. But he'd come for her at six and he wouldn't take no for an answer, she argued dismally. She'd committed herself to an evening with a host of strangers, all of whom would know each other and be decked up to the nines, and there she'd be—the proverbial Cinderella!

She stayed in the water until it was almost cold and she was beginning to resemble a shrivelled white prune, and then towelled herself dry too vigorously. Her ankle was turning all sorts of interesting shades, she noted with a detachment borne of thoughts of the evening, but at least it wasn't hurting so much and the swelling was beginning to slowly subside. She'd have to wear the bandage tonight, of course, but she just might be able to force a shoe on her foot.

She blow-dried her hair to the accompaniment of 'Hark, the Herald Angels Sing', courtesy of the radio, and then creamed herself all over to 'God Rest Ye Merry Gentlemen'. She had expected to feel abjectly miserable on this special day, or at least heartily melancholy, but with mouth-drying apprehension and quivering excitement vying for first place in her breast there was no room for anything else.

Creamed and dry, and still in her bathrobe, Marigold inspected the contents of the wardrobe and groaned weakly. She had packed with a view to a week or so in a remote cottage where warmth and comfort might be at a premium if there were power cuts or any other winter problems; not a top-drawer party!

She had brought her expensive tight black jeans—just in case everything else had got soaked through some catastrophe, not because she had thought she would actually wear them—but the only way they would look right for a party was teamed with a flamboyant top of some kind. And that she definitely did not have.

She frowned to herself, wondering if the cottage boasted a brown paper bag which would fit over her head and at least hide her mortification!

And then her eyes fell on the grubby lace curtain at the bedroom window. It might be dusty, she acknowledged as a dart of excitement shot into her mind, but if she wasn't mistaken it was the most beautiful antique lace in a soft cream. Dared she take it down and use it for tonight? She'd inherited her mother's flair with a needle and she always brought an emergency kit of needle and thread away with her; she could do this. She would buy the most fabulous replacement in the world after Christmas—not that Emma would probably even notice she had used the curtain in the first place. She had been talking about paying someone to come and clear the house—furniture, carpets, curtains and all—the last time they'd met when Emma had given her the key.

Marigold limped over to the window, reaching out a tentative hand and touching the lovely old material reverently. Funnily enough it wasn't Emma's reaction to her using the curtain which bothered Marigold, but her grandmother's. Her eyes moved to the faded wallpaper above the fireplace where a wedding photograph of a young couple was hung. Emma's grandparents, she'd be bound. She hobbled over to the fire, gazing long and hard at the young, smiling girl resplendent in the old-fashioned dress and veil, and deep, dark eyes set in a lovely, sweet face stared back at her.

Take it, they were saying. Use it, enjoy it. Hold your head high and let everyone know you are as good as them. You're your own woman, aren't you? You would have fought to stay where you wanted to be, wouldn't you? *Wouldn't you?*

'I would.' Marigold breathed the words out loud.

So we are sisters, separated only by time. Take the lace and make it into something beautiful…

Marigold had the most absorbing Christmas Eve afternoon.

After gently removing the curtain from its hooks, she washed it tenderly. It dried within minutes by the fire, and then, very carefully, she cut the lace to a pattern she'd drawn out on an old newspaper, humming along to a Christmas carol concert as she worked.

Several hundred tiny, neat stitches later the top was ready, and even to Marigold's critical eyes it looked like a million dollars. She pulled it over her head for the final fit and then sat, flushed with success, as she looked at her reflection in the ancient mirror on the back of one of the wardrobe doors. It could be a Dior, she told herself firmly. Or an Armani or a Versace. It had a real touch of class. And the simple black pumps she had stuffed into her case at the last minute wouldn't look amiss either. Of course, black strappy sandals would have looked better, but no one would have expected that with her ankle the way it was.

It was getting dark outside by the time she dressed the little tree Flynn had brought, but once festooned in the tinsel and glittering baubles Bertha had sent it looked delightful.

Marigold was so pleased with the top and the tree she had a glass of Flynn's wicked red wine with a calorie-loaded pizza at five o'clock, but, owing to the fact that she had resisted taking any of the painkillers with the party in mind that day, she felt she could indulge.

Once she'd eaten, she concentrated on her make-up and her hair. After two attempts to put her hair up she stopped fighting and allowed it its freedom. It fell, shining, swinging and glossy, to her shoulders, its subtle shades complimenting her creamy skin and deep blue eyes, although Marigold herself was oblivious to its beauty. She stared anxiously into the mirror, wishing she could twirl and pin it high on her head to give the illusion of an extra inch or two to her height, but it was so fine and silky it defied pins and restraints.

After applying the lightest of foundations to her clear, smooth skin, Marigold brushed a little indigo-blue shadow on her eyelids and a couple of coatings of mascara on her lashes. A touch of creamy plum lipstick and she was nearly ready. She bit fretfully on her full lower lip as she surveyed her reflection, and then clicked her tongue in annoyance as lipstick coated her two front teeth.

After a tissue had removed the offending colour Marigold tried again, her heart fluttering like the wings of a bird. The top looked great, but what she would give for another five or six inches on her height was nobody's business!

Calm, girl, calm. She fixed tiny silver studs in her ears—the only earrings she had brought with her—as she wondered what on earth she was doing. This was as far removed from the cosy, quiet Christmas Eve she'd had in mind a few days ago as a trip to the moon! But it was happening… She breathed deeply and prayed for serenity. It was happening and all she could do was to get through the next few hours with as much poise and dignity as she could muster.

Why had Flynn asked her to the party? Was he really interested in her or was she just a novelty; worse, did he feel sorry for her? But those kisses hadn't been borne of pity, had they? No, they hadn't, she reassured herself feverishly. She might not be as experienced and worldly wise as Flynn Moreau, but even she knew the difference between sympathy and a far stronger emotion—that of desire.

But she didn't *want* him to desire her! The girl looking back at her from out of the mirror's misty depths challenged that thought with her bright eyes and flushed cheeks, and now Marigold's face showed a touch of panic. She had to get a grip on herself, for goodness' sake. A man like Flynn could have any woman he wanted with a click of his fingers; he wasn't about to lose any sleep over her one way or the other. All she had to do was to make it clear she wasn't on for a little Christmas hanky-panky and she wouldn't see him for dust. Simple really.

The firm, loud knock on the front door of the cottage interrupted this rational line of thought and brought Marigold's eyes snapping open to their fullest extent. He was here! She cast one last, frantic glance at the mirror and then shut her eyes tightly for a moment, before opening them and bringing back her shoulders in a stance which would have been more appropriate for going to war than to a Christmas Eve party.

She had rested her ankle all day and she felt the benefit of this as she walked to meet Flynn, although it had still been a slight struggle to force her shoe over her swollen foot.

'Hi.' His voice was lazy as she opened the door; his eyes were anything but.

Marigold flushed slightly at the male appreciation the grey gaze was making no effort to conceal, and knew every second of the hours it had taken to make the lacy top was worthwhile. 'Hello.' She was pleased how composed her voice sounded.

'You look beautiful,' he said very softly, his height and breadth accentuated by the dusky-grey silk shirt and black trousers he was wearing.

Marigold was overwhelmingly relieved he wasn't in a dinner jacket. Her top with the expensive black jeans came nicely within smart-casual category. Nevertheless, his clothes screamed an exclusive designer label. For a moment she had the slightly hysterical thought—borne of nerves—as to what he would say if he knew she was wearing an old curtain, but then she thrust it to one side and answered politely, 'Thank you.'

'Here.' He had been holding one hand behind his back and now he brought out a small box in which reposed the most exquisite corsage of two pale cream orchids. 'I must have sixth sense or something; it's just the right colour.'

'Oh, how lovely.' She was entranced at the delicate beauty of the flowers, the pink in her cheeks deepening at the unexpected gift. 'But you really shouldn't have.'

He smiled slowly, extracting the corsage from its snug box and bending forward to fix it on her top as he said quietly, his eyes on the flowers, 'Wilf's prepared one for each of the female guests tonight, courtesy of his greenhouse.'

His fingers were warm against her skin as he fixed the

orchids in place and Marigold was glad he was concentrating on the corsage for two reasons. One, his touch was doing the strangest things to her insides, and two, *ridiculously* the fact that every woman at the party was receiving the same gift had hurt for a moment.

'But I chose this one myself.' His voice smoky warm, he added, 'There was something about the delicate beauty on the outside of the flower married to the fierce, passionate colour within which reminded me of you.'

That suggestion again that she was passionate, fiery... Marigold wrenched her eyes from his as she looked down at the orchids, their scent heady and the rich, vibrant scarlet inside the graceful blooms a magnificent contrast to the cool loveliness of the exterior.

'That's very flattering,' she managed fairly lightly, 'especially for someone called Marigold Flower. I've never imagined myself being likened to an orchid.'

'Oh, I'm not underestimating the beauty of the marigold, I assure you.'

He was still very close, too close, and she didn't like how her nerves tingled but found her body's response was quite outside of her control.

'I think they're exquisite flowers, as it happens,' he continued silkily, his eyes intent on her flushed face. 'The French marigold with its yellow and chestnut-red flowers and the full, delicate African variety are just as lovely as the dwarf with its small single orange flowers, and they are all fighters, did you know that? Hardy and determined to survive as well as beautiful. Of course, they prefer sunny, tranquil places and a trouble-free existence, but when adversity and storms arrive they find they can grow almost anywhere.'

Marigold was quite aware Flynn was talking about more than garden plants. She stared at him, wondering how it was that the veiled compliments should give her such enormous pleasure when she had only known him for forty-eight hours or so. And then she took hold of the feeling of excitement and gratification as a little warning voice deep in her mind spoke cold reason. As a chat-up line it was pretty good and he had obviously done his homework on marigolds, she thought wryly, but all this didn't mean anything beyond a brief flirtation.

'You certainly know your flowers,' she said as off-handedly as she could manage.

'No, just marigolds.' He was watching her closely, seriously, and a little trickle of something she couldn't name shivered down her spine. And then the firm, stern mouth relaxed, a smile twisting along his lips. 'Come on, everyone will be wondering where we've got to,' he said evenly. 'Have you got a wrap or coat or something?'

She had only brought her fleece and cagoule with her and neither was remotely suitable for this evening, Marigold thought distractedly as she hurried back to the bedroom. But other than freeze she had no choice but the fleece; she hadn't even brought a cardigan with her—just several chunky jumpers.

She reached for her black purse, which she'd emptied of money a few minutes earlier and replaced with a lipstick and comb, and caught a glimpse of herself in the mirror as she did so. The tight black jeans, waist-length lacy top and black pumps *did* look good.

She glanced at her faithful old fleece, which had seen better days, and decided to freeze.

Flynn was using the snowboard that had been propped against the wall of the cottage to clear the path when she locked the front door and popped the key into her purse, so the walk to the big 4x4 parked just outside the garden gate was problem-free.

Marigold paused before climbing into the vehicle, glancing up at the sky, which was now clear of snow clouds. A host of twinkling diamonds set in black velvet stretched endlessly in the heavens, timeless and enchanting, and below the frost had already formed crystals on the surface of the snow like a carpet of diamond dust. It was a beautiful, *beautiful* Christmas Eve, Marigold thought wonderingly. And she was going to spend it in the company of this commanding, enigmatic man, Flynn Moreau.

And the strange thing, the really fanciful thing was that she'd been fighting a feeling all day that somehow this was meant to be. Fighting it because she knew, in the heart of her, that a man like Flynn would be treating this as a pleasant interlude, no more. And because every instinct she possessed was screaming the warning that he was a dark threat to her peace of mind, her well-being, and if she let just the tiniest chink in her armour fail she would regret it for the rest of her life.

CHAPTER SIX

IT WAS halfway through the evening—when Marigold admitted to herself that she was having the time of her life—that she found she could actually smile at her ridiculous notions concerning Flynn. Of course, by then she had downed several glasses of the champagne that seemed to be flowing as freely as water, but that had only relaxed her a little, she told herself firmly. Flynn's friends were a great bunch and they had welcomed her as if they had known her all their lives, and Flynn himself was a charming host.

The house was a Christmas dream, decorated with traditional holly and ivy and deep-red velvet ribbons, and the enormous Christmas tree standing in the hall was a vision of red and gold, tiny flickering candles and shimmering baubles vying with streams of glittering tinsel and fairy lights.

Marigold found she was never alone, even though she had refused several offers to dance because of her ankle. Somehow she'd been drawn quite naturally into a group of Flynn's colleagues who were about her age or a little older. As the evening progressed she found they were wonderful company, funny and often outrageous, teasing each other with a naturalness that declared they all knew each other very well.

Flynn seemed to be near by even when he wasn't actually with her most of the night, but his attentiveness—if that was what it was—was merely the kind that a good host would display to a guest who didn't really know anyone else, Marigold reminded herself umpteen times during the evening.

At midnight there were howls of excited laughter and little shrieks when Father Christmas, complete in red suit and white beard, appeared, delving into his enormous sack for presents for everyone. All the women had items of jewellery and the men gold cuff-links, and as Marigold unwrapped her gift—a pair of tiny gold hoops with a single red stone enclosed in a teardrop hanging from them—she happened to glance at Flynn, intending to mouth 'thank you' across the heads between them.

He was leaning back against the wall close to where she was sitting, arms crossed over his chest and a faintly brooding expression on his dark face, and for a disquieting moment she got the impression he was viewing them all from a distance, like a scientist forced to inspect some rather uninteresting bugs under his microscope.

Marigold felt the impact of the thought like a shower of cold water and lowered her eyes quickly, making an excuse about visiting the cloakroom in the next moment and escaping from the noisy throng.

Once in the cloakroom, which had been designated for use by the ladies only, the gentlemen having to use one on the floor above, Marigold went into one of the two cubicles and closed the door, needing some privacy to marshall her whirling thoughts. Flynn's whole charming, amenable-host act had been nothing more than that—an act, she told herself flatly. None of them had seen what the real man was thinking or feeling tonight. That look on his face; it had been unnerving, disturbing.

Marigold glanced down at her ankle, which was beginning to remind her it was still around, and breathed deeply several times to control her racing heartbeat. It was what she had sensed in him all along, this autonomy. The women had been flocking around him tonight and even the men searched out his company, obviously enjoying his companionship, but all along he had been... What? she asked herself. And the answer came, absent from them. Flynn was here in the physical but mentally a million miles away.

She sat in the cubicle for a few moments more, angry with herself that the revelation had bothered her so much. All this would seem like a dream when she got back to the reality of her life in London; none of it mattered, not really.

And then, as though to call her bluff, she heard the door to the cloakroom open and the sound of voices.

'But who *is* she? Surely someone knows?'

'Darling, you know as much as me. According to Flynn she's a friend, that's all. She's staying in that dear little cottage we pass to get to the house apparently.'

Marigold had intended to rise and leave her hidey-hole but had frozen at the first words, knowing they were talking about her.

'Friend? Well, there are friends and friends!' The other woman giggled, not nastily but in a way that brought a pink tinge to Marigold's cheeks.

'Janet! You're terrible. You don't know anything's going on, now then. Anyway, don't forget there's always Celine in the background,' the other woman warned in a much more sober fashion. 'Whoever this girl is and whatever the relationship between her and Flynn, she'll go the same way as the rest.'

'He's such a dreamboat, though, isn't he?' Janet sighed, long and lustily. 'One night with Flynn and I bet you'd be ruined for any other man.'

'Janet!' Now Marigold could tell the other woman was definitely shocked although she was half laughing when she said, 'You've only been married six months; you should still be in the first throes of married bliss and thinking only of Henry! Right, that's my face repaired; are you coming?'

'Yes, all right. Let me just put on a bit more lipstick…'

There was a brief pause before the sound of the door opening and closing again, and then silence.

Marigold sat absolutely still for a full minute. Celine. Whoever this other woman was, she would have to be called something like that; something more ordinary just wouldn't fit the bill. Celine, Tamara… Were they born with names like that or did they choose them themselves when they decided to turn into *femmes fatales*? So, Flynn had a Celine in his life, did he? A Celine who he always returned to, by the sound of it.

Marigold stood up slowly, anger beginning to replace the sick feeling of disappointment. He'd had no right to kiss her when he was involved with someone else. 'Whoever this girl is and whatever the relationship between her and Flynn, she'll go the same way as the rest.' The woman's words burnt in Marigold's mind.

Clearly Flynn and Celine had one of these open relationships, or perhaps the other woman just put up with the status quo because she knew she was different to a casual affair? That she had his heart if not exclusive rights to his body?

Marigold looked down at her hands and realised her fingers were curled into her palms so tightly they were hurting. She forced herself to relax them finger by finger, took a deep breath and then opened the door of the cubicle, stepping out into the carpeted area where the two washbasins reposed against a mirrored wall. It was quite empty.

She splashed her wrists with cold water for a few moments before dabbing some on the back of her neck. She had no reason to feel angry and let down, she told herself miserably, but she did. He had only kissed her a couple of times when all was said and done.

And then she frowned. No, this line of reasoning was flawed, she declared militantly to herself. Flynn had told her he was a single man, and maybe he was—technically. But with Celine around, in her book he was definitely not up for grabs. Not that she would have grabbed him anyway, Marigold reassured herself fiercely. But the fact remained he had not been totally honest with her, even if he *had* told everyone she was just a friend. At least those gossipy women hadn't been sure if there was anything between her and Flynn. Which, of course, there wasn't, never had been and never would be, Celine or no Celine, she added vehemently.

So…she would go back out there and behave just as she had been doing all evening. She'd laugh and joke and be friendly, and when Flynn took her home—*if* he took her home; he might well get Wilf to do the honours, for all she knew—she would thank him politely for a wonderful party and make a graceful exit out of his life. And that—*most definitely*—would be that. She would be quietly dignified and decorous, and would never intimate she knew anything at all about Celine. He was entitled to live his life exactly as he chose, but as far as she was concerned she thought it stank!

She stood a moment or two more, staring at herself in the mirrors. She would make it abundantly clear she did not fancy him or want anything at all to do with him; if nothing else he would remember her a little differently from *the rest*. Those words had got right under her skin, she admitted ruefully. There was something terribly humiliating in being herded under such a heading.

She applied fresh lipstick, ran her comb through her hair so it fell in shimmering wings against her soft skin, and then squared her shoulders.

Right, Flynn, she thought with a trace of dark amusement. This is where you start having to face the fact that you are not God's gift to the whole female race!

Couples were dancing to a popular Christmas hit in the hall as she made her way back to the drawing room, edging carefully round gyrating bodies. Still more were jigging about on the perimeter of the drawing room and the buzz of conversation and laughter was deafening. Everyone was having a wonderful time.

'I missed you.' Flynn must have been waiting for her because no sooner had she put her nose through the door than he was at her side, the intensity of his gaze making her skin burn in spite of herself.

'Oh, I doubt that.' She forced a light laugh she was inordinately proud of.

'Then I'll have to convince you somehow,' he murmured softly, smiling his slow smile. 'Let's find a quiet corner.'

Oh, no, she wasn't having any of this. If he wanted a Christmas intrigue—Celine obviously being elsewhere—he had picked the wrong girl, Marigold told herself tightly. She flashed him a brilliant smile. 'I wouldn't dream of taking you away from your other guests,' she said brightly, turning away from him in the same instant and making her way over to the group she had left earlier, inwardly seething.

Those two women had known about Celine and no doubt the existence of the other woman was common knowledge among the rest of the folk here, or a certain number of them at any rate. How *dared* he come on to her in front of everyone?

She had half expected Flynn to follow her and press his cause, but when there was no firm male hand on her shoulder or soft voice in her ear she assumed he hadn't thought it was worth the effort—that *she* wasn't worth the effort.

The talk within the group had shifted to medical matters when she rejoined them, several of the party being doctors and nurses. One of the other women—married to a young surgeon who was just relating the complications he'd encountered when he took the appendix out of some unfortunate soul—leant across to Marigold as she sat down. 'It always turns to work,' she murmured conspiratorially. 'If I've heard about one operation at a dinner party or some function or other, I've heard about hundreds! It's so boring. Oh, sorry, I never thought— you're not in the profession, are you?'

'Not me.' Marigold smiled back into the rosy face topped by blonde curls. She had noticed this particular couple earlier; the wife was about seven months pregnant and always laughing and cuddling her doctor husband, and he was blatantly besotted with his pretty wife. Marigold had found herself envying them with all her heart, which had surprised her at the time. Even when she had been engaged to Dean she had been in no particular rush to settle down and have babies, and now that was definitely on the back burner. But something about this couple had made her terribly broody. It must be wonderful to be pregnant by the man you love, she thought with a sudden painfulness which amazed her afresh.

'Good, I'm glad you're not a doctor or nurse. We can talk fashion and hairstyles and soaps—*anything* but hos-

pitals and operations!' The pretty face smiled at her and
Marigold smiled back, forcing herself to concentrate on
the conversation rather than do what every nerve in her
body was willing her to do and to turn round and see
where Flynn was.

At one o'clock Bertha appeared with hot mulled wine
and a stack of mince pies and a Christmas cake which
would have fed a small army, and at half-past one the
first of the guests began to leave—some to their rooms
within the house, and others to the village inn some
miles away where Flynn had apparently booked rooms.
According to Marigold's new friend, those guests staying at the inn were returning in the morning for
Christmas lunch and tea.

Flynn had joined the group some fifteen minutes or
so after Marigold but he hadn't singled her out for any
special attention, keeping everyone amused with a dry,
wicked wit that could be slightly caustic, and which had
everyone—Marigold noted with acid cynicism—hanging
on his every word. He was clearly the big fish in this
particular pond, and the other guests' adulation—which
bordered on reverence in Marigold's jaded opinion—
grated unbearably.

'The offer's still open for you to use the annexe tonight.' Marigold had walked across to the laden trolley
at one side of the room to leave her glass and empty
plate with the others deposited there, and she hadn't been
aware Flynn had followed her until his deep voice
stroked across the back of her neck.

'No, thank you.' She tried, she *really* tried to keep her
voice light and friendly, but even to her own ears it
sounded strained.

'OK, out with it, Marigold,' Flynn said coolly.
'What's the matter?'

'The matter?' She nerved herself to turn and face him, wiping her face of all expression. 'Sorry, I don't understand. I thought I'd made it clear yesterday I intended to sleep at the cottage?' And definitely, *definitely* not in his bed. If he thought he could use her as a bed warmer till Celine turned up, he'd got another think coming.

'Forget where you're sleeping. I asked you what was the matter.'

She stared up at him, at the stern mouth and firm jaw, and it was with deep self-disgust that Marigold realised she envied Celine more than she would have thought possible. 'Nothing is the matter,' she lied steadily.

'Marigold, part of the job of being a good surgeon— and I am a damn good surgeon—is to know when people are tense and worried, when they're keeping something back,' he said evenly. 'Something has happened tonight and I want to know what it is.'

The arrogance was outstanding. Marigold looked him squarely in the eye. 'Just because I don't want to stay in your house—' or sleep in your bed '—doesn't mean there's anything the matter,' she said firmly, hidden desperation helping the lie to trip more easily off her tongue. 'I'm tired, that's all, and I want to go back to the cottage, but I've had a lovely time and thank you for asking me.'

She sounded for all the world like a small child primed by her mother to thank the hostess at the end of a birthday party. Flynn's eyes narrowed as they moved over her uplifted face. 'So you'll be joining us for lunch tomorrow?' he asked silkily.

'Thank you but no. The ankle's really sore tonight so I'll probably spend most of the day in bed.' Lying the second time was easier, she realised detachedly.

Flynn nodded, his face holding all the warmth of a block of cold granite. 'I'll take you back to the cottage.'

'Oh, right.' Somehow she hadn't expected him to capitulate so swiftly. She'd won, she told herself silently as she said goodbye to everyone and made her way with Flynn to the front door, so why did it feel as if she'd lost?

Once they were sitting in the big vehicle she knew it was because she *had* lost. One or two couples who were obviously staying at the inn had followed them outside into the clear, icy air, and now their cars roared off into the freezing night, but Flynn made no effort to drive away after starting the engine.

Marigold turned to him after a few seconds had ticked by with excruciating slowness.

'We aren't budging until I get the truth,' he said pleasantly. 'There's a full tank of petrol and we can sit here all night with the engine running to keep us warm. *Are* you warm enough?' he added.

She was absolutely frozen but would sooner have walked on red-hot coals than admit it. 'I'm fine.'

He didn't actually call her a liar—reaching into the back seat and lifting over a thick car rug was eloquent enough—but Marigold didn't put up a protest when he wrapped it round her; her teeth were chattering too much.

It was a full five minutes before anyone spoke again, and the silence had got so loud it was deafening, when Marigold—warm again, buried as she was in the soft folds of the rug—said tightly, 'This is perfectly ridiculous, you know that, don't you? People will wonder what on earth we're doing out here.'

'I've lived for thirty-eight years without caring what people thought; I don't intend to start now.' He'd shifted in his seat to face her when she had spoken and his voice was perfectly calm.

Now, that was probably the most honest thing he had said to her since they'd met, Marigold thought bitterly. 'So you live by your own codes and values, regardless of anyone else, do you?' she flung back, goaded into saying more than she had intended.

'I wasn't aware I'd said that.'

'But it's the truth,' she stated fiercely. 'Well, I'm sorry but I happen to believe in monogamy within a relationship for as long as it lasts.'

His eyes narrowed. 'Meaning, I presume, that I don't?'

'Are you saying you do?'

'Whoa, lady.' He had been affable up until a moment ago; now the handsome male face was as cold as the scene outside the window and his eyes were steely. 'I'm getting the distinct impression I'm being set up for a fall here, and I don't intend to defend myself to you or anyone else.'

What a very convenient attitude, Marigold thought hotly.

'Now, I don't know what's going on in that pretty head of yours, but for the record I think fidelity is the foundation for any man-woman relationship, whether the parties intend it to be a permanent one or not. Does that answer your question?'

Oh, the *hypocrisy* of it! Marigold was so mad she forgot all her noble intentions. 'And Celine?' she asked icily. 'Does she hold to your views and still kiss every man in sight? Or perhaps fidelity in your book is something different to the dictionary definition?'

For a moment there was absolute stillness within the vehicle, her words seeming to hover in the air and echo all about them, and even before Flynn replied Marigold knew something was desperately wrong. She'd made a terrible mistake.

She braced herself for the explosion that was sure to come if the look on his face was anything to go by, her stomach muscles knotting and her mouth suddenly dry.

'Celine?' His voice was quiet, expressionless. 'Who spoke to you about Celine and what was said?' His very quietness was more intimidating than any outward show of rage.

'No one; it wasn't like that. They didn't know I was there. In the cloakroom...' Her voice trailed away; she was making a mess of this. But he hadn't denied there was a Celine. She took a deep breath and said quickly, 'I was in the cloakroom and two women were talking. They said...' She stopped abruptly, trying to remember the exact words.

'Yes?' One word but painfully chilling.

'They said Celine was always in the background, even when you...when you were with someone else,' she faltered uncomfortably, wishing with all her heart she had never started this.

'What else?'

'Nothing, not really. Just that it sounded as though there had...well, been quite a few...'

'Affairs?' he put in ruthlessly.

'Yes.' Well, it *had* sounded like that. 'All the rest'. How else could she take that?

'So you assumed from this snippet which you overheard that I have a lover but indulge in brief affairs with other women when the fancy takes me. Is that it? And you did not think it pertinent to ask me about it? You preferred to freeze me out all night?' he grated softly, looking as though he would like to shake her or worse.

Marigold stared at him. What had she done? Oh, what had she done? 'I...I didn't freeze you out—'

'The hell you didn't,' he said grimly, starting the engine as he spoke and then swinging the large vehicle so violently round the drive in a semicircle that Marigold nearly screamed.

The set of his jaw warned her to say nothing more as he drove—far too fast in view of the treacherous conditions—back to the cottage. Marigold sat hunched in her seat, her mind numb and all her senses concentrated on getting out of the vehicle in one piece.

By the time they drew up outside the garden gate Marigold felt weak with relief that they weren't in a ditch or wrapped round a tree, and as Flynn left the car she just managed to pull herself together sufficiently to shrug off the rug before he opened the door, holding out his hand to help her down.

She glanced at his coldly impassive face. 'Thank you.' Her voice was very small but as she descended he said nothing, merely holding her arm as she limped along the path, which was now a sheet of ice.

She had to have two tries at sliding the key in the lock before her trembling hands could negotiate the point of contact, and once the door swung open he turned and began to walk away. Marigold stared after him, her heart racing, and knew she had to say something, *anything*. She couldn't just let him go like this. 'Flynn?' Her voice was shaking.

He stopped but didn't turn round. 'Yes?'

'If I got it wrong, I'm sorry. Truly. But they made it sound...' Her voice trailed away. 'I'm sorry,' she said again.

'You believed what you wanted to believe,' he said flatly.

Marigold opened her mouth to deny it but the words hung on her tongue unsaid. He was right. She stared at the big figure in front of her, appalled. He was absolutely right. There could have been all manner of explanations for what she'd overheard, but she'd jumped to the obvious one because she had needed to distance herself from this man. From the moment she had met him he had been a threat somehow.

When she remained silent he swung to face her, and now a mirthless smile twisted the hard mouth briefly as he read the truth on her face. 'Don't worry, I won't bother you again; you can have your quiet Christmas,' he said wearily, turning and walking on down the path again.

'Flynn?' She had no right to ask and it was probably the height of presumption in view of all that had been said, but she would never sleep again if she didn't *know*. 'Who is Celine?'

For a second she thought he was going to ignore her but then he halted again, his back to her as his voice said flatly, 'Celine was my fiancée; you may have heard of her—Celine Jenet?'

Marigold *had* heard of her; there probably wasn't a woman in the western world who hadn't heard of the beautiful French model.

'We were together for a while some years ago but we parted a week before the wedding. It caused a great deal of interest at the time; probably, in view of what you heard tonight, it still does.' There was a biting note of cynicism running through the cold voice now. 'It deeply disappointed the media, and to a lesser extent our friends and families, that we didn't choose to tell all or rip each other apart, but at the risk of sounding tedious we were friends. We still are, but that's all we are.'

Marigold didn't know what to say but in the event it didn't matter because Flynn obviously considered the conversation finished. He walked on, climbing into the vehicle without even a nod of his head or a wave of his hand.

Long after the lights of the 4x4 had disappeared Marigold continued to stand on the doorstep, only entering the house when she became aware she was chilled to the bone.

Celine Jenet. She sank down onto the rug in front of the glowing fire in the sitting room, removing the guard she had put in place before she left for the party and placing several small logs on the red embers, which leapt into immediate, crackling life. *Celine Jenet.* She was gorgeous. Six feet of sultry, large-eyed, tousled sex-kitten appeal, and she had been his fiancée. No wonder those women had said no one else could match up to Celine. Why had she left him? For another man? Because of her career maybe?

Marigold stared into the flames, her heart thudding. Whatever the reason, it had not caused Flynn to hate Celine, but did he still love her? He had said they were only friends but that didn't mean he didn't secretly wish for more, perhaps even hoped they might get back together some day.

She held out her cold hands to the fire but found the chill came from within rather than without. Flynn might not hate his ex-fiancée but it was a sure-fire bet he hated her, Marigold thought miserably. And now she thought about it, especially in view of his explanation about the Frenchwoman, she didn't understand why she had behaved so badly. She didn't normally jump to erroneous assumptions about people; in fact she was just the opposite. If she hadn't given Dean the benefit of the doubt on various occasions she would have realised what he was up to long before she had. But with Flynn...

With Flynn it was different. For some reason this man affected her like no other human being she had ever met.

Marigold bit hard on her lip, hating the way she was feeling but unable to conquer the utter desolation that had swept over her. So much for a quiet, peaceful Christmas by herself to recharge her batteries and get strength to face the changes she intended to make in the future. She wished she'd never set eyes on this cottage, or Flynn, or—

The knock at the door startled her so much that for a second she was in very real danger of overbalancing into the fire. She put a hand to her thudding heart, rising quickly and limping across the room and into the hall. She went right up to the front door, her voice small and cautious as she said nervously, 'Who is it?'

'Father Christmas, who else?' Flynn's voice said sardonically.

Flynn! Marigold opened the door with a certain amount of embarrassment, her head whirling. She hadn't expected to see him again and she'd been amazed how badly that had made her feel, but now he was here she was warning herself, This doesn't mean anything, not a thing. After Celine Jenet, how could it?

As the door swung open Flynn just stood and looked at her steadily for a moment or two before saying, 'Hello, Marigold. Can I come in?'

'Oh, yes, of course.' She was so flustered she hardly knew what she was doing and was quite unaware she'd kept him standing on the doorstep.

Once they were standing in the sitting room she had the presence of mind to say quickly, 'Can I get you a drink? A glass of wine, or coffee or hot chocolate?'

'Coffee would be great.'

'Right.' She could feel her cheeks burning and desperately needed a few minutes to compose herself away from his searching gaze.

'Can I help?' he asked softly, for all the world as though the last caustic hour hadn't happened.

'No, you sit down,' she said a little weakly. 'I won't be a minute.'

By the time she'd prepared a tray with the coffee-cups and a plate of biscuits, Marigold's colour had subsided though the secret excitement and nervous agitation bubbling away in the depths of her hadn't.

Flynn was sitting on the sofa in front of the fire when she walked back into the room with the tray, and he appeared perfectly relaxed, one knee crossed over the other and his arms stretched along the back of the cushions. It was a very male pose, but she had noticed that about him—every movement, every gesture was overwhelmingly masculine. If Flynn was a man who was in touch with his feminine side, he hid it very well.

'I just want to say I really am very sorry for jumping to conclusions about…about what I heard,' Marigold said before she lost her nerve, setting the tray down on the little table Flynn had obviously placed in front of the sofa before he sat down.

'You believe me, then?'

'Of course I do.' He looked incredibly sexy sitting there, his eyes veiled and his countenance expressionless, and a shiver trickled hotly down Marigold's spine, curling its way into the core of her.

'There's no ''of course'' about it,' he said evenly. 'But I realised once I'd left that I'd expected a hell of a lot. You were in a crowd of people, none of whom you knew, and you hear a little idle talk from people who

should have known better. The thing is—' he paused
abruptly, his jaw clenching, before he continued '—my
private life is just that—private—and I don't appreciate
it being under discussion. It's of no interest to anyone
but me surely?'

Now, that was expecting too much, especially of the
female of the species, Marigold thought as she stared
back into the handsome face. Looking as he did and with
the air of remote detachment he had about him, let alone
the sort of work he did, where his skill and expertise
was the difference between life and death, gave him a
fascinating power and magnetic appeal which was irre-
sistible to any hot-blooded woman.

The thought sent a wave of unease trembling through
her as it hammered home her own attraction to Flynn.
She didn't want to be attracted to him; she didn't want
to be attracted to anyone for years and years until she
had worked through the Dean and Tamara thing in her
mind. But Flynn, with his abundance of male aggression
and sexual appeal—he was the last man on earth to get
involved with, however fleetingly.

Marigold plunged in before she had time to weigh her
words and chicken out of what she knew she had to
make clear. It still seemed incredible that Flynn might
be interested in her, albeit mildly, but just in case…
'Flynn, what you said earlier, about me believing what
I wanted to believe? Well, you were right in a way,' she
said feverishly, standing just in front of him with her
hands clasped tightly together. 'It's just that after Dean
I don't feel I can cope with…with a new friendship,'
she finished weakly, aware the last few words sounded
ridiculous.

'I think we are both aware it wasn't altogether friendship I had on my mind.'

His voice was quiet but carried the velvet, smoky undertones she'd heard before and brought the colour which had recently subsided back to her cheeks again.

He was offering her an affair, a brief relationship, and probably from his point of view that was perfectly OK—certainly from what she'd overheard in the cloakroom he'd gone the same route many times before since Celine. But how did a woman bounce back after Flynn Moreau? Marigold asked herself silently as she looked into the rueful eyes fixed on her face. The others must have managed somehow, but she wouldn't. It would be a case of going from Dean's frying-pan into Flynn's fire, and she'd have no excuse with Flynn. She'd be walking into this relationship with her eyes wide open.

'The thing is...' She stopped, wondering how she could make him *see*. 'The thing is...'

'What is the thing?'

'Those...those women said you'd had other relationships since Celine, all temporary,' she managed at last. 'And that's fine,' she added quickly, 'if it's what you and your girlfriends wanted. But I don't think I'm like that, and it's too soon after Dean to even start thinking about... And you're wealthy and successful and always meeting new people and everything, and I'm—'

'Delightful.' He'd stood up, and as strong arms caught her against him she looked up into a hard male face that appeared mildly amused.

'Flynn—'

He cut off her voice by the simple expedient of taking her lips and as she stiffened, determined not to give in to the thrill of being in his arms again, the smell and feel of him surrounded her and she knew she was lost. The thing was, he kissed so *well*, she told herself helplessly. She had never met anyone who kissed like Flynn.

She sighed against his mouth and immediately, as he sensed her submission, the kiss deepened with masterful intent, his lips moving against hers and bringing forth a response she was unable to control.

She felt herself beginning to melt as before, and although his power over her senses was frightening it was so exhilarating she curved into him, hungrily searching for more. She had never considered herself a particularly cold person, but before Flynn lovemaking had been a mildly pleasurable experience at best, an irritation at worst when she hadn't really been in the mood.

But this, *this* was like something you read about in novels—mind-blowing, dazzling, and in spite of herself Marigold admitted to a feeling of excitement and satisfaction that she could actually experience such passion. Being in Flynn's arms like this made her feel desirable and wholly feminine, one half of a two-piece, flesh and blood jigsaw.

His mouth moved to the honey-tinted skin of her throat, nuzzling, caressing as she shivered with delight, her body arched backwards as he leant over her. He kissed her ears, her eyelids, tracing a scorching path back to her mouth, which opened obediently at his touch. His hands had moved under the lacy top, his fingers firm and warm as they stroked the silky skin of her narrow waist before moving upwards to run over the soft swell of the top of her breasts beneath her lacy white bra.

Her hands had splayed up into his thick black hair, her fingertips softly massaging his scalp in a sensual abandon which would have shocked her if she had been able to think coherently.

His mouth had parted her lips and he was tasting the inner sweetness with tiny darting movements, causing electric vibrations that had her trembling against him.

Marigold was enchanted, enchanted and beguiled, avidly searching for something she had never had but which she now sensed was within her grasp.

Flynn's breathing was heavy when he at last lifted his head, his lips releasing her mouth, but his arms still holding her close to him.

Marigold opened dazed eyes to find the silvery gaze fixed on her face, and for a moment she had the insane impulse to beg him to *really* make love to her; to follow her into the bedroom next door where they could lie on the big, soft bed with the glowing fire illuminating their naked bodies and all thoughts of the outside world banished.

It was enough to bring her out of the stupor and back down to earth with a bump. And he knew, instantly; the hungry, watchful expression on the hard male face changing to one of wry regret. 'You're doing it again,' he murmured softly.

'What?'

'Thinking instead of feeling.'

She moved back a little in his arms, pushing at the broad, muscled chest and he let go of her immediately. 'You don't approve of rational thought?' she asked in as light a voice as she could manage, considering she was feeling utterly bereft. 'I would have thought it was a necessity in your line of work.'

'There's a time and place for everything.' He smiled a slow, sexy smile and her heartbeat went haywire.

'Flynn—'

'I know, I know.' He interrupted her softly, tilting her chin to look into the deep violet-blue of her eyes. 'You aren't ready for a relationship. It's too soon. We're miles apart in lifestyles. Right?'

Marigold nodded shakily. 'Right.' In the space of

three days this man had turned her world upside-down. How had he done that? And in spite of all she had said if there hadn't been the mental image of Celine in the background, she wasn't at all sure that she wouldn't have thrown caution to the wind and just gone with the flow.

'Marigold, we both know that if I hadn't stopped a minute ago we'd be making love on the rug in front of the fire right now,' Flynn said in such a conversational tone of voice that for a moment she didn't take it in.

She stiffened, angry with him for telling the truth. 'If you believe that, why *did* you stop?' she challenged tightly.

'Because this is not the right time or the right place,' he returned silkily, 'and contrary to what you might think I consider that important. There's something between us you can't deny; it's been there from the first moment we laid eyes on each other and there can only be one possible conclusion to such raw physical attraction. But you have to accept me into your life before you accept me into your body, I can understand that, otherwise, being the sort of woman you are, you'd tear yourself apart.'

She stared at him, utterly bemused by the straight talking and the fact that he clearly considered an affair between them was just a matter of time. 'I can't believe you're saying this,' she said weakly.

'Why?' he asked casually, turning away and pouring them both a cup of coffee, before he added, 'Cream and sugar?'

Cream and sugar? Was he mad or was it her? He had just calmly stated that regardless of all she had said he intended to make sure he slept with her at some point in the immediate future, hadn't he? 'Flynn, you can't ride roughshod over all I've said,' she stated more firmly, ignoring the coffee tray.

'I wasn't aware I was,' he said mildly. 'I have taken into account all your objections but I have a predilection for the truth, Marigold, and it's the truth that you're really objecting to.'

Marigold looked at him in exasperation. He had an answer for everything! She opened her mouth to argue some more but then shut it abruptly. She'd never win in a war of words with Flynn, but then she didn't have to, not really. He had said he'd wait until she had accepted him into her life before pressing his case—at least that was what she thought he had said—and so it was quite simple really. She would be on her guard for the next few days while she was here in Shropshire, and then when she left, that would be that. No contact, no telephone calls or anything else. She'd be ruthless; she would have to be because Flynn was right about one thing. This physical attraction between them *was* raw and powerful, and far too compelling to play about with. For her at least.

'Cream and two sugars, please,' she said sweetly.

'What?' Marigold had the satisfaction of seeing him blink before he said, 'Oh, yeah, the coffee.'

And the coffee was all he was going to get, this night or any other, Marigold told herself firmly, even as a little voice in her mind reminded her nastily, until he chose to kiss her again...

CHAPTER SEVEN

WHEN Marigold awoke on Christmas Day it was to the realisation she had promised to have lunch and tea with Flynn and his friends, and she rolled over onto her stomach, pulling a pillow on top of her head as she groaned loudly. She was mad, quite mad!

Flynn had behaved perfectly for the rest of the time in the cottage the night before. He had drunk two cups of coffee, eaten most of the biscuits and made small talk, which had the advantage of being amusing and interesting. After inveigling her agreement regarding the next day he had given her a brief peck on her forehead and left immediately, leaving Marigold with the unwelcome—but faintly exciting—thought that Flynn was a man who would always get what he wanted.

After a long, hot soak in the bath Marigold inspected the meagre contents of her limited wardrobe. The black jeans would have to be utilised again, and a long, thick cream sweater with a large rolled neck would fit the bill for today. She felt a thrill of anticipation and elation shoot through her, and it was enough for her to spend the next hour or two warning herself she couldn't afford to let her guard down for a moment.

Flynn was the type of man who would whisk her into his orbit and keep her there for as long as it took for the attraction between them to burn itself out. And then? Then she'd be left floating in the middle of nowhere. It had been stupid to agree to go the house today, but this would be the last time she would concur with what he demanded. And there *was* a houseful of guests around. It wasn't as though they were there alone, she comforted herself briskly as she put the last touches to her make-up. It would be fine, just fine.

And it was. He came for her just after eleven o'clock and Marigold was ready and waiting, determined to give him no excuse to be alone with her in the cottage.

She hastily shut the front door as the big vehicle drew up outside the garden gate, her ankle allowing her to walk almost normally as she hurried down the snow-covered path.

Flynn had climbed out of the 4x4 and opened the passenger door as she reached him, her senses registering six foot plus of gorgeous manhood encased in black jeans and a black leather jacket. 'Hi.' His voice was soft and he grinned, dropping a quick kiss on her lips before he helped her up and closed the door behind her.

It took Marigold all of the drive to the house to get her racing heart under control, but his manner once they were there—warm and friendly and not at all threatening—relaxed her sufficiently to allow her to have a wonderful day.

Bertha, along with Wilf—whom the housekeeper had commandeered to help her—excelled herself with Christmas lunch, her pièce de résistance in the form of two enormous Christmas puddings, flaming with brandy and accompanied by lashings of whipped cream, bringing forth a round of applause from everyone at the dining table.

Replete, everyone played silly games all afternoon, although again Marigold noticed Flynn was more of a benevolent spectator than participator, and after a magnificent buffet tea they all gathered in the drawing room, where Flynn played the grand piano and everyone sang carols before the party broke up, and people began to leave for the drive home.

'I didn't know you could play the piano.' Flynn had tucked Marigold's hand in his arm, thereby conscripting her to stand with him on the doorstep, where he was watching his guests leave, and she spoke primly, trying to put things on a less intimate footing. With ninety-nine out of a hundred men, standing close like this would present no problems at all, but Flynn was the hundredth, as her racing pulse testified.

'There are a lot of things you don't know about me, Marigold,' he answered evenly, but with the smoky inflexion in his voice which gave it a sensual kick that was pure dynamite. 'Something I would be only too pleased to rectify, given half a chance.'

His eyes stroked her face for a moment before he looked down the drive again. 'I enjoy playing the piano and I'm told I can make a half-reasonable noise on the trombone. I like parasailing and scuba-diving; I prefer American football to English football or rugby and I loathe golf. But of course there are other...activities which give me more pleasure than all the rest put together.'

She didn't ask what they were, keeping her gaze on the car in front of them, from which the passenger was waving frantically, as she said, 'Scuba-diving? I've done a little of that, enough to get my PADI open-water certification.' She had tried to persuade Dean to do the course with her, thinking they could dive together in the warm waters of the Caribbean on their honeymoon, but he had only gone a couple of times before dropping out, claiming trouble with his inner ear. Privately she had thought he was scared. He had never coped well with a new challenge.

'So you're a water baby?' The moonlight caught the shining jet of his hair and turned the grey eyes to mercury as he turned to look down at her. 'That doesn't surprise me. I had you down as gutsy as well as beautiful.'

'Flattery will get you everywhere,' Marigold said as lightly as she could manage.

'I wish.' It was very dry. 'And it is not flattery. I told you before, I only tell the truth.'

'That would make you a man in a million,' she said with a trace of bitterness she couldn't quite disguise.

'Just so.' He smiled lazily. 'It's nice you've recognised the fact so quickly.'

And then he stiffened as he looked down the drive, his voice gritty as he said, 'Who the hell is that, driving like a maniac? He's just caused Charles to swerve and nearly go off the road. I don't recognise the car.'

Marigold followed the direction of his gaze and then swallowed hard. *She* recognised the car and it didn't belong to a him but a her.

Emma was driving the smart little sports coupé her doting father had bought her the year before, and she executed a flamboyant halt in front of the house which sent gravel scattering far and wide. 'Goldie, darling!' She was calling even as she unfurled herself from the leather interior. 'I've had a nightmare of a journey.'

'It's Emma,' Marigold murmured desperately. 'She wasn't supposed to arrive for another couple of days.'

'Lucky you.' It was caustic, antagonism bristling in every plane and line of his hard male face as narrowed eyes took in the tight leather trousers and three-inch stiletto heels, the dyed blonde hair and carefully made-up, lovely face.

'I was waiting outside the cottage and one of the cars

stopped and told me you were here,' Emma continued as she walked towards them, speaking to Marigold but with her big green eyes fixed on Flynn. 'Darling, I *had* to get away from London. Oliver and I have had the most *awful* row and I never want to see him again in all my life,' she finished dramatically, before adding, as though she had suddenly realised her lack of manners, 'Oh, I'm Emma Jones by the way,' as she held out one pale beringed hand to Flynn.

He made no effort to reach out and take it, merely nodding as he said, 'Maggie's granddaughter. It figures.'

Emma stopped abruptly. She was used to men going down before her shapely figure and batting eyelashes like ninepins, not having them growl at her with a face like thunder. However, Emma was made of sterner stuff than she looked, and her voice didn't falter as she said, 'What exactly does that mean?'

'I was a friend of your grandmother's and cared about her; I think that says it all.'

'Really.' Emma lifted her small chin and slanted feline eyes, but it was obvious she knew exactly what Flynn meant when she said, 'Daddy said there were some rather rude individuals in this neck of the woods.'

'Daddy was right. And this particular rude individual is now asking you, politely, to get off his property,' Flynn said evenly.

At some point during the discourse Marigold had disentangled her hand from Flynn's arm and now she said hurriedly, 'I'll get my bag if you want to wait in the car for me, Emma.'

'Sure.' As Emma turned and began to saunter away Marigold fled into the house, grabbing her bag from where she'd left it in the drawing room and retracing her footsteps into the hall, where she found Flynn waiting for her.

'You don't have to go.'

'I do.' Marigold bit her lip. 'You know I do.'

'Can I see you tomorrow?' he said quietly.

'I don't think that's a good idea.'

'I disagree,' he said, still very softly. 'It's an excellent idea.'

'Please, Flynn—'

'What are you so scared of anyway, Marigold? Is it me? As a man, I mean? Or is there something more? Something in your past concerning this ex-fiancé of yours? Did he ill-treat you in any way?'

'You mean apart from sleeping around in a way that ensured everyone knew but me?' Marigold asked derisively, and then she paused, taken aback at her own bitterness. Right up until this moment in time she hadn't realised how deep the wound had gone, and for a second she hotly resented Flynn forcing her to see it. She didn't want to think of herself as damaged or a victim, she thought furiously. She had to get the victory over this.

'I have to go.' She gestured towards a scowling Emma, sitting looking at them from the gently purring coupé. 'Emma's waiting.'

'Damn Emma.'

'I have to go.' She backed into the doorway and out beyond, running to the car in a way that played havoc with her injured ankle.

Once Marigold was inside the car, Emma wasted no time in leaving, her speed indicating quite clearly she was mortally offended even if she had handled the situation with surprising coolness. *'What an awful man!'* They hadn't got out of the drive and onto the lane beyond the gates before Emma let rip. 'How dare he talk to me like that? And what were you doing in his house anyway?'

'I beg your pardon?' OK, so Emma might be upset but no way was she going to apologise for being in Flynn's home. 'I wasn't aware it was out of bounds,' Marigold challenged quietly.

Emma sent a swift glance Marigold's way and her tone was less confrontational when she said, 'Of course it isn't; I just wasn't aware you knew the owner, that's all.'

'I don't—I didn't,' Marigold corrected. 'It happened like this…' She explained the circumstances of her first meeting with Flynn, leaving out his comments relating to Emma and her family and finishing with, 'I think he thought quite a bit of your grandmother, Emma.'

Emma shrugged offhandedly. 'I barely knew her,' she admitted indifferently. 'I know she drove my parents mad with her refusal to go into an old people's home, and that she had a load of flea-ridden animals, but my father usually visited her on his own.'

'How often was that?' Marigold asked quietly.

'Now and then.' It was cursory. 'She had plenty of friends hereabouts.'

'It's not like family though, is it?'

'Don't *you* start.' Emma skidded to a halt by the side of Myrtle and Marigold could almost see the small car flinch as the sports car missed her bumper by half an inch. 'My grandmother had the chance to go into a home where she would have been looked after and which my parents could have visited more easily, but she insisted she wanted to stay in the cottage. My father is a busy man; he's got an important job. He can't waste time running about all over the place, besides which he and Mother entertain a lot—important people, necessary for his position at work. Anyway, they didn't get on, my grandmother and father. Just because my father was unable to attend my grandfather's funeral, my grandmother said she'd never forgive him.'

'Why couldn't he go to the funeral?' Marigold stared at Emma's disgruntled face and wondered why she'd never realised that she really didn't like this girl at all.

'Pressure of work,' Emma said perfunctorily. 'You have to make sacrifices if you want to get to the top.'

'Yes, I suppose you do.' Marigold opened her door as she added, 'I'm leaving in the morning, Emma; there are things I need to do at home. Are you still intending to sell the cottage?'

'I might be.' Emma glanced at her as they walked to the cottage door whereupon Marigold handed the other girl the front-door key. 'Why?'

'I'd be interested in knowing how much you want for it, that's all.' Somehow she couldn't bear the thought of Emma owning the beloved home of the young, sweet-faced bride in the photograph, or selling it to someone who wouldn't appreciate the blood, sweat and tears old Maggie had put into the last years. 'Along with the furniture, the pictures, everything,' she added quietly.

'All that old rubbish?' Emma looked at her as if she was mad, and she probably was, Marigold admitted wryly to herself. 'Whatever would you be interested in that for?'

'It fits the cottage, that's all.'

'Doesn't it just!'

Marigold slept the night on the sofa in the sitting room despite Emma's insistence that she could share the bedroom, and by nine o'clock the next morning she was on her way back to the city. If she had stayed any longer there would have been a very real possibility of her and Emma having a major fall-out, and she didn't want that. Not so much because it would make things difficult at work as because she felt old Maggie was relying on her to buy the cottage and make it a real home again.

It might be fanciful, Marigold admitted as her car chugged cheerfully along, this link she felt she had with Emma's grandmother, but she felt it in her bones and she couldn't get away from it.

As she drew nearer to London, Marigold found she couldn't stop Flynn from invading her thoughts as he'd done all night; his image in her mind seemed to increase with the miles. He had accused her of being scared of him; was she? she asked herself, hating the answer when it came in the affirmative. She had run away this morning, she acknowledged miserably; for the first time in her life she had run away from something—or, more precisely, someone. Admittedly she would have left the cottage after her conversation with Emma; it had grated so much she couldn't have stayed and pretended everything was all right as far as the other girl was concerned, but she should have popped to see Flynn on the way and told him she was leaving. After all he had done for her it would have been courteous if nothing else.

But… She gritted her teeth at the but. She'd known deep in the heart of her but not admitted till now that she'd wanted to see him too much as well as not at all. How was that for a contradiction? she thought ruefully.

Was she thinking of buying Emma's cottage because it would mean Flynn would be her neighbour? Marigold tried to take a step backwards and answer her question honestly. No, she didn't think she was, which was a relief. But neither did Flynn's presence just across the valley make her think the notion was impossible, which, if she wanted nothing at all to do with him, wasn't sensible, was it?

Oh, this is crazy, stupid! Why was she tearing herself apart like this over a man she hadn't known existed a week ago? He probably wouldn't give her another thought once he found out she'd gone—if he bothered to enquire, that was.

Marigold honked Myrtle's horn long and hard at a smart Mercedes that cut her up from an approach road and felt a little better for letting off some steam.

If her buying the cottage worked out—great. If it didn't, so be it. Either way she'd still put her plans for the future into operation and go self-employed. One stage of her life was finishing, another was just beginning, and it was up to her what she made of things.

She was not going to think of Flynn Moreau any more. He was a brief interlude, a little bit of Christmas magic maybe, but Christmas was over, as was her flirtation with Flynn. She nodded resolutely to the thought and then, as she caught the eye of the passenger in the car alongside, pretended to be nodding along to a song. Look at her, she told herself crossly once the car had changed lanes and disappeared, she was going barmy here! Enough was enough. Decision made. Autonomy for the immediate future and definitely, *definitely* no men in her life.

Marigold spent the next two days of the holiday cleaning her small flat in Kensington from top to bottom, and catching up with several domestic jobs she had been putting off for ages. She didn't allow herself to think, keeping the radio or TV on at all times and ruthlessly curtailing any stray thought which crept into her consciousness and might lead down a path to Flynn.

She returned to work on Wednesday morning with her notice already typed and in her bag. Patricia and Jeff were sorry to accept her notice but promised her work on a freelance basis, and after she'd agreed to stay until the end of March all parties were happy. Emma was on holiday until the new year and Marigold wasn't sorry, despite her desire to set the ball rolling with regard to her purchase of the cottage. The other girl's callous attitude about her grandmother had bothered Marigold more than she would have liked.

The first day back at work was quiet, what with quite a few firms having taken an extended break until after the new year, so for once Marigold left the office on time and was back home before six o'clock. The phone was ringing as she walked into the flat; it was her mother, insisting she join the rest of the family and friends for a New Year's Eve bash at her parents' home.

After promising her mother she would think about it—an answer Sandra Flower was not particularly happy with—Marigold managed to put down the phone some twenty minutes later; her mother having bent her ear about everything from her cleaner's bad leg to the state of the nation.

Marigold hadn't taken one step towards the kitchen for the reviving cup of coffee she'd been literally tasting for the last few minutes, when the front doorbell rang followed by an imperious knock a second later.

'Give me a chance...' Marigold grumbled to herself as she went to the door, pushing back her shining veil of hair with a weary hand. The hard physical work in the flat over the last two days, added to the twinges her ankle still gave which kept waking her up in the night, had caught up with her after a day at work and she was looking forward to a long, hot soak in the bath with a glass of wine, followed by an early night.

'Hello, Marigold Flower.'

It was Flynn. Bigger, more handsome and twice as lethal as she remembered, his dark hair tousled by the strong north wind which had been blowing all day and his grey eyes narrowed and faintly wary. He looked tired, she noticed with a detachment borne of shock. Exhausted even.

Marigold said faintly, 'How did you know where I lived? Emma didn't…?'

'No, Emma didn't,' he assured her drily. 'Let's just say Emma took great pleasure in slamming the door in my face and leave it at that.'

'You *were* awful to her,' Marigold said weakly, still trying to take in the fact he was right here on her doorstep.

'She got off damn lightly and she knows it.' Flynn was dismissive.

'So how *did* you find me?'

'Process of elimination. There aren't too many M. Flowers in London, and your number was about the fifth my secretary tried. Your answer machine provided the name Marigold…' Dark eyebrows rose above brilliant eyes. 'Do I get invited in?' he asked softly.

'Oh, yes, of course.' She was so flustered she nearly fell over her own feet as she quickly stepped to the side and ushered him through.

'I've been in London for the last thirty-six hours,' he continued quietly. 'Emergency call from the hospital.' And then he stopped in the doorway of her small sitting room, glancing round appreciatively as he said, 'This is charming.'

'Thank you.' Marigold had spent every night for a

month painting and papering her tiny home in the immediate aftermath of the break with Dean, needing the hard work as therapy to keep her from caving in to the pain and rage and bitterness. She had gone for bright, bold colours to offset her internal bleakness, and the sitting room with its radiant yellow walls reminiscent of sunflowers and pinky terracotta sofa and curtains on a pale wood floor was daring and adventurous. 'I like it.'

He turned to her, his grey eyes smiling. 'It suits you.'

Oh, wow, he was something else. Impossible, dangerous and more attractive than any man had the right to be. Marigold sternly took hold of her wildly beating heart and said evenly, 'Why are you here, Flynn?'

'To see you.' He stated the obvious with a wry smile. 'You never said goodbye, remember?'

'You came here to say goodbye?'

'Not exactly.' he pulled her against him, bending quickly and kissing her with hard, hungry kisses that brought an immediate response deep inside her. He kissed her until she was limp and breathless against him and then raised his head, his voice slightly mocking as he said, 'No, not exactly, but then you knew that, didn't you? Just as you knew I'd follow you.'

'I didn't!' she said indignantly, her voice carrying the unmistakable ring of truth.

He frowned, tilting her face upwards with a firm hand. 'Then you should have,' he said softly, without smiling.

Probably, but then she wasn't versed in all the intricate games of love like his more experienced women friends. She was just herself; a not very tall, rather ordinary, hard-working girl with the unfortunate name of Marigold Flower. And she dared not let herself think this could mean anything.

'I came to ask if we could try getting to know each

other for a while,' he said smoothly, reading the confusion and withdrawal in her face with deadly accuracy. 'OK? No heavy stuff, just the odd date now and again when I'm in town. Dinner sometimes, a little sightseeing, visits to the theatre, that sort of thing. Just being together with no strings attached.'

She stared at him uncertainly. What exactly did all that mean? Did the dinner dates end up in bed? Was that part of the getting to know each other? 'As...as friends?' she asked shakily.

He looked down at her with a wry expression which made him appear twice as handsome. 'Is that what you want?'

She nodded quickly. 'I'm not ready for anything more.'

He was still holding her chin in his warm fingers and now his gaze intensified, pulling her into its mercurial depths until she felt he was drawing her soul out for inspection. And then, quite unexpectedly, he smiled his devastating smile, drawing her against the hard wall of his chest so that his chin was resting on the top of her head. 'Good friends,' he qualified lazily.

The warmth of him, the smell and feel was sending her heady, and over all the surprise and shock and uncertainty was an exhilaration and excitement that he had sought her out, that he was *here*. And she was glad. Too glad. 'I'll make some coffee.' She drew away slightly and after one moment of holding her close he let her go.

'I could use some.' He stretched powerful shoulders beneath the big overcoat he was wearing. 'It's been a hell of a day. A bad accident is never pretty but when the injured party is only eight years old it takes on a different picture.'

'The emergency call?' she asked quietly. His voice

and face had changed as he'd spoken, and suddenly his exhaustion was very evident again.

'Uh-huh.' He shook his head wearily. 'And it could have been prevented if the parents had checked the boy was strapped in. How can you expect an eight-year-old to remember seat belts when he's taking his new remote-controlled car to show his grandparents?'

'But he's going to be all right?'

'Two major operations in the space of thirty-six hours and two pints of blood later, yes, he's going to be all right. But it was touch and go for a time and we came damn near to losing him more than once.'

'You haven't been working for thirty-six hours?' she asked as the reason for his exhaustion really hit home.

'More or less.' He shrugged offhandedly. 'It's an all-or-nothing type job.'

He was an all-or-nothing type guy. 'Have you eaten yet tonight?' Marigold thought gratefully about the extensive spring clean of the last couple of days and the sparkling fridge newly stocked with food.

He shook his head. 'I think I ate some time yesterday but it's been coffee and biscuits in short bursts today. I was going to suggest I take you out for dinner if you're free?'

She stared at him. He was dead on his feet. 'Did you drive here?' she asked quietly.

'Taxi.'

'In that case I'll get you a glass of wine while you take off your coat and make yourself comfortable,' she said briskly. 'Lime and ginger pork with stir-fried vegetables OK?' It gave her great satisfaction to see the way his eyes opened in surprise. She might not be a Bertha, but she could still rustle up a fairly edible meal when she wanted to.

'That would be great,' he said softly, the tone of his voice bringing a tingle to her skin. 'If you're sure?'

Sure? She hadn't been sure of a thing since the first time she had laid eyes on Flynn Moreau! 'Quite sure.' She smiled in what she hoped was an efficient, I'm-totally-in-control type of way, walking across to the little living-flame gas fire and turning it on full blast as she said, 'Sit down and get warm. Red or white wine?'

'Red, please.'

He was shrugging off his overcoat as she turned, and the perfectly ordinary, non-sexual action sent nerves racing all over her body. It was worse when she returned from the kitchen with the wine. He had clearly taken her at her word regarding comfort. His suit jacket was off and he'd loosened his tie so that it hung to one side of his pale grey shirt, the top buttons undone to reveal the dark shadow of body hair on his upper chest as he stood inspecting a photograph of her parents.

For a moment Marigold forgot how to walk, and then she managed to totter over to him without spilling anything. 'Your parents?' he asked, inclining his head at the photograph.

Marigold nodded, handing him his glass of wine as she said, 'It was taken last year.'

His eyes returned to the picture of the entwined couple; the man grey-haired and somewhat sombre as he stood with his arm tight round his laughing wife, who was petite and sparkling.

'I like it because it sums them up very well,' Marigold said softly with a great deal of love in her voice. 'Dad is a solicitor and very correct and proper, and Mum—well, Mum's not,' she admitted ruefully. 'But they think the world of each other.'

'It shows. Are you close to them?' he asked as he raised his eyes, watching her.

'Yes, I think so. Perhaps not quite so much in the last little while since I moved out and got a place of my own, but that change was necessary as much for Mum as me,' Marigold said quietly. 'She always wanted lots of babies but there were complications after me. Consequently I became the focus of all her attention and because we're very different that caused problems at times. But we're fine now. She accepts I'm an independent adult with my own way of doing things…mostly,' she added with a smile. 'How about you? Do you see much of your parents?'

'Not much.' He turned back to look at the photograph as he said flatly, 'They divorced when I was five, got back together when I was eight and divorced again when I was approaching my teens. They've had several marriages between them since then. My mother married Celine's father when I was eighteen, which is when Celine and I met for the first time. It was her father's third marriage.'

Marigold didn't know what to say.

'Our parents lasted three years but by the time they divorced Celine and I were close. We understood each other, I guess, having had the same sort of fragmented childhood.'

Marigold nodded. It hurt more than she would have thought possible to hear the other woman's name on his lips, which was a warning in itself.

'I was brought up in an atmosphere of too much money and too little purpose.' He was speaking more to himself now than her. 'I needed to break the cycle before it broke me, hence the medical profession. I could put something back there, you see, do something lasting.

The idealism of youth.' He glanced at her, a cool smile twisting his mouth. 'And it turned out that by some fluke I found my niche. I was a good student, and neurology had always fascinated me. The rest, as they say, is history.'

Marigold wanted to ask him more about Celine; when they'd realised they'd fallen in love; when they'd got engaged; what had caused the break-up. But she realised the brief glimpse into his past was over when he raised his glass, his voice changing as he said, 'To Maggie.'

'To Maggie?' She stared at him in surprise as she raised her own glass.

'Of course. Without the cottage being left to Emma we wouldn't have met, so we have Maggie to thank for it.'

'If Emma hadn't suggested I use it for Christmas we wouldn't have met,' she corrected factually.

'If you think I'm toasting Emma, think again.' He grinned with a sexy quirk of his sternly sensual mouth and she acknowledged defeat.

'To Maggie,' she agreed quickly, taking a great gulp of wine for much-needed support before she backed away from him, saying, 'Sit down and relax while I see to dinner. The remote for the TV is on the coffee-table,' before she turned tail and fled into the fragile safety of her small kitchen.

Once the oven was on and she had placed the pork loin steaks in the roasting tin, Marigold quickly made the glaze, mixing together lime rind and juice, soy sauce, honey, garlic, ginger and the other ingredients before she poured the mixture over the chops. She popped the tin into the oven and finished her glass of wine, pouring herself another before taking the bottle and walking into the sitting room to see if Flynn wanted a refill.

He was half lying in a somewhat awkward position on the sofa, as though the onslaught of sleep had caught him unawares—which it probably had, Marigold thought dazedly through the frantic beating of her heart. One hand was thrown back over his head and the other was still round his empty glass, and she was breathlessly aware she was seeing him vulnerable and defenceless for the first time.

He looked different in sleep; younger, more boyish, the deep lines round his eyes and mouth less pronounced, and his thick dark eyelashes adding to the illusion of youth. Not so his body; the broad, muscled torso and powerful thighs spoke of a man in his prime, and even sleep couldn't negate the flagrant maleness that was an essential part of his appeal.

Marigold moved forward, she couldn't help it, even though part of her was objecting that if their positions had been reversed and she had been asleep she would have hated Flynn being able to examine her at leisure.

His suit was beautiful and clearly wildly expensive, as was the silk shirt and tie, but he had looked just as good in the old jeans and sweater he'd worn to bring in the Christmas trees, she thought faintly.

She looked at his mouth, relaxed now but still so sexy it made her want to put her own lips against it, and at the hard, square male chin where black stubble was clearly visible.

What would it be like to be made love to by this man? Even the thought of it made her weak at the knees. The firm power of his naked flesh, the warmth of his body heat, the delicious and unique smell of him encompassing her in wave after wave of exquisite pleasure...

She knelt down by the sofa, telling herself she only wanted to remove the glass from his nerveless fingers and put it safely on the coffee-table, where she could fill it with wine ready for when he awoke.

This close, his aura of masculinity was disturbingly sensual, the combination of brooding toughness and little-boy susceptibility almost painful. She took the glass very slowly, easing it out of his fingers and placing it on the floor by the side of the sofa without turning to the coffee-table. She found she couldn't tear her eyes away from the sleeping face. His childhood, the break with Celine, the things he saw every day in his work must have all contributed to the cool, distant, cynical expression which veiled his countenance when he was awake, but like this she could almost imagine those things had never happened.

She touched the rough male chin very lightly with her lips, she couldn't help herself, and when there was no response, no stirring, she dared to move upwards to the firm mouth. She had never found over-full lips attractive on a man and Flynn's were just right; cleanly sculpted and warm. She shut her eyes for just a moment, knowing she had to move away and return to the kitchen, and when she opened them again silver orbs were staring straight into shocked violet.

She seemed to be incapable of doing anything but look back into his gaze, shock freezing her reactions, but then his arms came round her and she found herself drawn upwards and onto him so that she was lying half across the big, powerful frame. 'Nice...' It was a contented male murmur and he was holding her so closely, so securely, there was no point in struggling. She didn't want to anyhow.

His mouth teased at hers as he stroked over her compliant, soft body, exploring her curves and valleys with a leisurely enjoyment that sent tiny thrills cascading down her nerves and sinews. Languorously her head fell back to expose the curve of her throat as his mouth searched lower, and then it returned to her lips, the kiss more urgent as he made a low, deep sound of satisfaction in his throat.

It was as he moved her hips, drawing her against him in a manner that guaranteed she couldn't fail to become aware of his body's arousal, that she became aware of what she was allowing. She stiffened, but immediately he sensed her withdrawal, his voice soft and husky as he said, 'It's all right, sweetheart, it's all right. I'm not an immature boy who is going to insist on more than you want to give. Relax...'

'I...I have to see to the dinner.' She sat up, her voice breathless, and he made no effort to hold on to her by force.

'Damn the dinner.' But his voice was lazy rather than annoyed.

'I brought you some more wine.' She stood up quickly, her cheeks flushed as she endeavoured to straighten her clothes and brush back her tousled hair.

He sat up straighter himself. 'That's very kind.' It was mildly amused, and made Marigold feel about sixteen years old.

'The glass is by your feet.' She stepped back a pace as she spoke. 'Help yourself to the wine. I'll just go and see to the vegetables or the pork will spoil.'

'Heaven forbid.'

She gave a weak smile and scurried into the kitchen, furious with herself. How could she have kissed him like that? she asked herself angrily as she took out her aggression on a hapless onion, slicing it with savage intent. After all she had said about being friends she practically had to go and eat the man! Talk about sending mixed signals. And she just *hated* women who did that.

Did he call all his women sweetheart?

The thought came from nowhere and stopped her dead, and she stood for a full thirty seconds, staring at the carrots waiting nervously for her ministrations after they had seen her behaviour with the onion.

And then she shook herself irritably. It didn't matter if he did or not, she told herself firmly. By his own lips he was just going to ask her out on the occasional date when he was in town in order that they could get to know each other a little better. She thought of the hard, hot arousal she had felt against the soft flesh of her belly before she had sat up, and her cheeks burnt with brilliant colour.

Their getting to know each other had taken a giant step forward all of a sudden, but that had been her fault, not his, she reminded herself honestly. The poor man had been utterly exhausted and fast asleep and she'd leapt on him like a raving nymphomaniac!

She groaned faintly before taking a long, hard gulp of the wine, just as the poor man spoke from the kitchen doorway, his voice somnolent. 'Need any help?'

'No, I'm fine.' She slung the onion into the oil heating in her large frying-pan and went to work on the carrots without turning round. 'I'm sorry I woke you,' she added quickly. 'I didn't mean to. I was only going to pour you a glass of wine...' Her voice trailed off. Buy that, buy anything.

'I'm glad you did—wake me, that is.'

She could feel his eyes on the back of her neck and she just knew the wretched man was grinning, although she didn't dare turn round. 'As you're awake now, could you perhaps set the table in the sitting room?' she asked primly. Her little pine table was tucked away in a small alcove and she rarely used it except when she had a guest, but it was just the right size for two. 'You'll find mats and glasses and everything in that cupboard.' She turned and pointed to the wall cupboard by the kitchen door as she spoke, studiously avoiding his eyes.

'Sure thing.'

Which was probably exactly what he thought *she* was tonight after the little scenario in the sitting room, Marigold thought tightly.

However, once she had served up the pork and vegetables ten minutes later, garnishing the aromatic food with fresh slices of lime, she had calmed down sufficiently to face him with a bright smile as she walked into the sitting room, carrying the two plates.

'Wow!'

She had cooked plenty—he'd had the look of a hungry, as well as exhausted, man—and her reward was in seeing his face light up at the sight of his loaded plate. 'Hazelnut pie and ice cream for dessert—shop-bought, I'm afraid,' she said lightly. 'Or there's some cream rice pudding I made yesterday if you prefer?'

'Got any strawberry jam to go with the rice pudding?' he asked hopefully, totally unsettling her again as he pulled out her chair for her to be seated before sitting down himself.

None of her other boyfriends, Dean included, had treated her with such old-fashioned courtesy, and it was very nice—too nice. She didn't dare get used to it. Not that Flynn *was* a boyfriend, of course, she clarified silently. 'Strawberry jam? I think so.'

'Great.' He grinned at her and she wondered how many of his female patients fell in love with him at first sight, or whether there were any who took a little longer.

Whether it was because Flynn put himself out to relax her or the two glasses of red wine she had consumed on an empty stomach Marigold didn't know, but she found she thoroughly enjoyed the rest of the evening.

The meal was leisurely, finishing with coffee and brandy after dessert, and Flynn was nothing more threatening than an amusing, agreeable companion who regaled her with fascinating and often hilarious stories about his life and work. She had the sense to realise he was giving her the success stories and upbeat moments, and that there was a darker side to his work, but she just went with the flow, enjoying every second. Much of his humour was self-deprecating and it was a surprise to find he could poke fun at himself, mocking his position and status and the esteem in which he was held. It was also very endearing, and more than once Marigold had to take a hold of her susceptible heart.

When he made noises about leaving round eleven o'clock Marigold braced herself for a passionate goodnight kiss, or even maybe the veiled suggestion that he could be persuaded to stay given half a chance. Instead Flynn rang for a taxi and put on his jacket and coat, kissing her once—but very thoroughly—before walking to the front door.

'Will you let me buy you dinner tomorrow as a thank-you for tonight?' he asked softly as they stood on the threshold.

Marigold nodded; the kiss had left her breathless.

'Eight-ish?'

She nodded again.

'Goodnight, sweetheart.'

And he was gone.

CHAPTER EIGHT

THAT night was the first of many spent in Flynn's company. He wined and dined her, taking her to the theatre, to various nightclubs, to parties and for meals out with his friends.

If he was in London at the weekends they would browse in art galleries and book shops, go for long walks along the Thames or spend the day at the private gym and leisure centre of which Flynn was a member. Lunch at charming, out-of-the-way places; tea at the Ritz; dinner at the Savoy—they did it all, and not once in the weeks leading up to the beginning of March did Flynn act as anything other than attentive escort and charming friend.

It was driving Marigold mad.

It was useless to tell herself that he was acting this way because *she* had insisted upon it, that she'd laid down very definite rules and boundaries because of her conflicting emotions where Flynn was concerned, and that this was the best, the very best way to proceed.

Every time he took her hand or pulled her against him, every time he kissed her goodnight or sat with his arm round her or stroked her hair, she waited for him to make the next move. And he didn't. He just didn't!

Most nights, and especially following the evenings when she saw him, Marigold tossed and turned for hours before she could fall asleep, her mind racing and her body burning. She tried to convince herself her restlessness was due to all the changes occurring in her life, and there were plenty of those.

Emma had agreed to the sale of the cottage as soon as she had returned to the office in January. Apparently she had had a dreadful time there; being unable to light the fires without filling the cottage with smoke, struggling with the ancient stove and blocking the sink were just a few of the mishaps she'd suffered.

The final straw had occurred when a mouse had decided to investigate the bedroom one night, Emma had reported, and then added insult to injury by choosing one of Emma's sheepskin slippers for a nest.

In view of the isolation of the cottage and not least Emma's new-year decision to travel round Europe for a while with one of her friends, purportedly to recover from her broken heart at Oliver's exit from her life, the asking price for the small house was very reasonable. A sizable bequest by Marigold's maternal grandparents some years ago which she had resisted touching until now meant she could afford a fifty-per-cent deposit on the cottage, and after she had shopped around a little she found a bank who were prepared to put up the rest. The deposit meant her mortgage repayments were gratifyingly low, and, with Emma including all the furniture and household effects right down to her grandmother's dustpan and brush, her immediate outgoings would be negligible.

Marigold had given notice she would be vacating the flat at the end of March, which was when she intended to move to Shropshire, and had printed myriad copies of her CV with an accompanying letter explaining she intended to freelance in her new location, and sent them to every contact she'd ever made. To date she'd had several promising replies which could lead to work in the near future but, apart from the partners at her present firm promising they would continue to leave the new designs for the greeting cards in her capable hands, nothing concrete.

And then, at the beginning of March, several events happened within the space of twenty-four hours and with a speed which left Marigold breathless.

At ten o'clock on a blustery March morning the cottage finally became hers; at eleven o'clock she was contacted by a small firm on the borders of Shropshire who had been given her name by their parent company in London. Would she be interested in a new project they were considering regarding a range of English countryside calendars, cards, diaries, notelets, et cetera?

Indeed she would, Marigold answered enthusiastically.

They would market the proposed venture very much on the lines of a 'local country artist' thrust, which was why she had been approached. They understood she was moving to Shropshire shortly?

At the end of March, Marigold confirmed, her heart beating excitedly.

Her CV stated Miss Flower had already had the experience of setting up a new section within her present firm. If their scheme was successful—and they had every reason to think it would be, as their parent company was intending to back them to the hilt—would Miss Flower be prepared to think about spearheading the development of this work?

Miss Flower would be only too delighted!

At three in the afternoon of the same day the telephone on her desk rang for the umpteenth time. Marigold picked it up, a lilt borne of the happenings of the morning in her voice as she said brightly, 'Marigold Flower speaking.'

There was a brief pause before a male voice said quietly, 'Marigold? It's Dean. I...I wondered how you were?'

'Dean?' If the person at the other end of the line had been the queen of England she couldn't have been more taken aback.

'Don't put down the phone.'

His voice was urgent, and Marigold wrinkled her brow before she said, 'I wasn't going to.'

Dean must have taken her honest reply as some form of encouragement, because he said with intensity, 'I've missed you. Hell, I've missed you more than words can say. I was such a fool, Marigold. Can you ever forgive me?'

She held the telephone away from her ear for a moment, staring at the receiver blankly. And then she said, 'It happened and I found it hard at the time, but it's in the past now, Dean.'

'But do you forgive me?'

Did she? Marigold considered for a second and realised she'd barely spared a thought for Dean and Tamara in the last two months. 'I've moved on,' she said steadily, 'so that must mean I forgive you.'

'I'm not with Tamara any more. She drove me mad half the time. Always wanting attention and never satisfied with anything. She wasn't like you, Marigold.'

Two spoilt brats with egos to match. No, she could imagine things might not have gone too well.

'I know I hurt you but there's never been anyone like you, you have to believe that,' he said softly. 'You've always been my anchor, the one person I could count on.'

She had to stop this. She didn't want to be anyone's anchor, she wanted far more than that, and she realised with absolute clarity that Dean would never be able to give of himself. Dean was what mattered to Dean. 'Dean, if things had been right between us you wouldn't have gone with Tamara in the first place,' she said steadily. 'It was just as well we found that out before we got married.'

'No, no, that's not it at all.' He sounded desperate and she was surprised to realise she felt sorry for him. It was like listening to a child, a selfish child who had broken his toy in a tantrum and was now demanding that it be put back together. But the toy had been an engagement, a commitment to get married. Flynn had said she could die waiting for Dean to grow up and he had been absolutely right. She had done her stint of babysitting him.

'It was your decision to go off with Tamara,' Marigold said firmly, hating the conversation with its distasteful connotations. 'And frankly I think it was the best thing for both of us. You obviously weren't ready for marriage and it would have been a disaster. There'll be someone for you in the future, Dean, but it won't be me. Goodbye.'

She put down the phone on his voice, her heart thudding fit to burst. It rang again almost immediately but she didn't pick it up, letting the answer machine click on. 'Marigold? Pick up. Please, Marigold, pick up.' A few seconds' silence followed, and then his voice came again, a petulant note creeping in as he said, 'I know you're there. Look, if you want me to grovel I will, but you know we're meant to be together. You love me, you always have done. I need you.' A few more moments of silence and then the receiver was replaced at the other end.

Marigold became aware she was holding her breath and let it out in a big sigh. Six months, and he expected he could pick up where he'd left off all that time ago at the drop of a hat. It would be laughable if it wasn't so tragic.

She sat staring at her paper-strewn desk, her mind racing on. He hadn't once asked her if she was with anyone—that clearly hadn't crossed his mind! It was incredible, but he thought she had sat at home just waiting for his call since they had finished! He didn't know her at all, but then she hadn't known him either. Which was scary.

It wasn't the first time she'd thought along these lines and the faintly panicky, disturbed feeling which always accompanied such reflections brought her nibbling at her lower lip. There *were* people who got it right and stayed together all their lives—her parents were a prime example—but there were plenty who got it terribly wrong, as she would have done if she'd married Dean. How on earth did you know if something was going to last or not?

She took a sip of the coffee Emma had brought everyone a few minutes before the call from Dean had come through, and grimaced. Somehow Emma managed to make perfectly nice coffee taste like dishwater! The thought of the other girl led her mind on to the cottage and then Flynn, and she knew her previous deliberations had nothing at all to do with Dean and everything to do with Flynn. She was in too deep. She liked him too much. This getting to know each other as friends hadn't been such a good idea after all.

She stood up restlessly, walking across to the big plate-glass window and looking down into the busy London street beneath. Dean had hidden his real self from her and she hadn't had the experience or where-withal to recognise the signs of his deceit. But compared to Flynn, Dean was like a little boy, so how on earth could she ever know where Flynn was coming from? She had made one big, big mistake with Dean; she didn't need to make another. Even without the spectre of Celine forever hovering in the background, Flynn Moreau was way, way out of her league.

All the excitement regarding the cottage and the wonderful offer of work faded, and she had the ridiculous urge to burst into tears. Instead she turned away from the view, marching back to her desk and attacking her mountain of paperwork with resolute grimness. No more thinking; no more ifs and buts. She had work to do.

She left the office later than usual, and almost got blown away by the wind as she stepped onto the pavement outside the building. There was a storm brewing, a bad one, she thought as she raised her eyes to an angry sky.

She did some shopping on the way home to the flat, struggling into the street of three-storey terraced houses with her arms feeling as if they were being pulled out of their sockets. She had just put the bags on the doorstep, delving into her handbag for the front-door key as the wind howled and the darkness surged all around her, when a hand on her shoulder nearly caused her to jump out of her skin.

'Sorry, did I make you jump?'

'Dean!' She'd swung round and knocked one of the bags full of groceries flying, and as they scrabbled about retrieving the food she said tightly, 'What on earth are you doing here? I thought we'd said all that needed to be said this afternoon.'

'I had to come.' He straightened with the bag of shopping clasped in his arms, and as she stared at him Marigold wondered why it was she had never noticed how weak his mouth looked. He was good-looking, in a boyish, charming manner, but almost... What was the word? she asked herself silently. Foppish. That was it. He was almost too well-dressed, too well-groomed. *And she'd planned to marry this man.*

'Dean, there's no point to this.' She held out her hand for the bag but he ignored it. 'Please, just go.'

'You don't mean that.' He moved closer, causing her to step backwards until she was pressed against the front door. 'You can't. We're meant to be together.'

The hell they were! The words sounded so like something Flynn would have said that Marigold blinked, as though she'd heard his voice. 'It's taken you long enough to find that out. It was the end of August we split, wasn't it?'

He stared at her, taken aback by her tone. He had clearly expected her to fall into his arms in grateful surrender after he'd made the big gesture of coming to her, Marigold thought grimly. She was relieved to find she didn't feel a shred of emotion at seeing him again beyond mild irritation. Hearing his voice so unexpectedly this afternoon had been a shock and it had upset her a little, raking up all the trauma. Now, faced with Dean himself, she knew he meant nothing to her any more.

'I'll make it up to you, Dee.' His pet name for her was annoying but that was all. 'I promise.'

He was still amazingly sure of himself, although Marigold thought she had detected just the slightest edge of uncertainty behind the arrogance, which made it all the more surprising when he suddenly lunged forwards, his free arm grabbing her as his mouth descended on hers.

For a moment Marigold was too startled to react, but then out of the corner of her eye she was aware of a vehicle pulling up on the road below them. She knew who was inside. Even before her eyes met ones of silver ice, she knew it had to be Flynn. It was fate, kismet.

She pushed Dean away, her voice sharp as she said, 'Don't! Don't touch me.'

'But Dee…' And then, as he saw her eyes were focused on something beyond him, Dean swung round, the shopping bag still in his hand. And then he saw the stony, cold face looking at them.

Marigold saw the metallic gaze take in what appeared to all intents and purposes a cosy shopping trip, and with the kiss on the step she half expected Flynn to order the driver to pull away.

Instead the door swung open and Flynn unfolded himself from the rear of the taxi cab, his height and breadth swamping Dean's slim five feet nine. 'Hello, Marigold.'

If one hadn't been looking into his dark, angry face, Flynn's voice could have appeared perfectly normal, Marigold thought a touch hysterically.

'I just stopped by for a quick visit,' he continued with the softness of silk over steel, 'but I can see you're otherwise engaged.'

In spite of the fact that Marigold was aware how bad it looked, she found she bitterly resented Flynn's assumption that she had been a willing participant in the kiss. And it was the knowledge of her own contrariness which made her voice brittle as she replied, 'Dean was just leaving, as it happens.'

'Really?' Flynn acknowledged the other man for the first time, his eyes scathing as they flicked over Dean, and in spite of the awfulness of it all Marigold knew a moment's amusement at the scandalised expression on her ex-fiancé's face. Dean had just had a salutary lesson in the fact that he was replaceable, and she hoped it might prove a warning to him in his dealings with the opposite sex in the future. 'Don't let me keep you,' Flynn said with distant chilliness, before his gaze returned to Marigold.

There was no further attempt at persuasion. Dean thrust the bag at her, his face like thunder, before he disappeared off down the street without a backward glance.

'That was Dean,' Marigold said weakly. She suddenly had the nasty feeling she had a tiger by the tail.

'So you said.' It was acidic.

'I didn't know he was going to be here. He phoned me this afternoon and then just turned up on the doorstep. I didn't...I mean I didn't want...' She stopped abruptly.

'Are you trying to say you didn't ask him here or invite him to kiss you?' Flynn asked evenly.

'Yes.' Which was stupid really because in view of the way she felt it would have been the easy option to let Flynn assume there was something between her and Dean, and thereby finish this 'friendship'. Flynn was not a man who understood the concept of sharing!

'Good.' He walked up to her, oblivious to the taxi driver, who was watching developments with interest. 'I'm pleased.'

'You believe me?' she asked weakly, astonished.

'Of course I believe you.' He smiled, a wry twist of his stern mouth. 'Didn't you expect me to?'

'I...' Her voice trailed away. She didn't know what she'd expected. 'I—'

'OK, I can draw my own conclusions.' He kissed her swiftly, lifting her chin with warm, firm fingers before adding, his voice very dry, 'I can see there is still some progress to be made.'

'What?'

But he was walking towards the taxi driver, bending down as he asked the fare and paying the man with what was obviously a handsome tip from the way Marigold heard the other man thank Flynn.

She watched him, her feelings so turbulent she hardly knew herself. She cared about this man and he was going to break her heart if she didn't finish this affair now, tonight. He had invaded her life with deadly intent, and even now she asked herself, why? He could have any woman he wanted—apart from the one who held his heart, Celine—so why bother with her? Was it because she'd made it plain she wanted nothing to do with him in the beginning, or just the way they had struck sparks off each other, mentally as well as physically? Right from the first time she had seen him it had been a love–hate relationship.

Her thought process hiccuped and died, leaving her in a state of suspended animation as she stared at the big figure in front of her. And then, as reason returned in a hot flood, she told herself, You don't! You do *not* love Flynn Moreau.

But it was too late. The truth she had been subconsciously denying for weeks was out in the open. Marigold wasn't aware of the blank despair which had turned her eyes navy blue, she only knew she mustn't betray herself by word or gesture.

'He's upset you.' Flynn was in front of her again, his handsome face unsmiling as he took in her drawn countenance. 'What's he been saying?'

'Who? What?' Marigold made an enormous effort and

pulled herself together. 'No, it's fine, really. He…he just told me he and Tamara have broken up. He wanted…'

'I think I know what he wanted,' Flynn said drily. 'And you told him to go paddle his own canoe, right?'

'My phraseology was a little different, but basically, yes.'

'You won't regret it.'

No, she wouldn't. Not with Dean. 'Flynn…' It was too soft, too trembling and feminine. She had to appear more in control. Marigold took a deep breath and her voice was firmer when she said, 'Flynn, we have to talk. About us, I mean.'

'There's an us?' One eyebrow quirked and his mouth lifted at the corners in a sexy smile. 'And I didn't know!'

'Please, Flynn.'

Something in her voice stilled the smile. His head tilted, eyes surveying her searchingly before he said, 'Inside. It's too cold and windy out here to deal with life and death issues.'

Once in the flat Flynn deposited the shopping he'd insisted on carrying in on the kitchen worktop, before walking through to the sitting room, where Marigold had just lit the fire.

'So.' He had on his big charcoal overcoat, undone, over an expensive grey suit and cream shirt, and looked every inch the powerful, dynamic and brilliant surgeon. He folded his arms over his chest, leaning against the wall just inside the door as he surveyed her unblinkingly. 'Let's have it.'

Please let me get through this without bursting into tears or disgracing myself in any other way, Marigold prayed desperately. I can't be with him on his terms, and any other way is out of the question. 'I think we ought to have a break from seeing each other,' she said stiffly, rising from where she'd been kneeling in front of the fire and seating herself on the sofa.

'Why?'

'Why?' Well, of course he would ask that, she told herself crossly as she heard her voice echo his. She just didn't have a reasonable answer, that was the thing. 'Because I'm not ready for a relationship so soon after my engagement finishing,' she attempted quickly.

'Don't buy it,' he said coolly. 'What's the real reason?'

She didn't answer immediately and his eyes narrowed. 'The truth, Marigold, and I shall know if you're lying,' he said softly.

'I...I'm not like your other women.'

He gave her a hard look. 'Flattering though some men might find it to be compared to a sultan in a harem, I'm not one of them. I wasn't aware I had ''women'' plural.'

'You know what I mean.'

'No, Marigold, I do not know what you mean. If you're insinuating I conduct my love life like a bull let loose in a field of cows—'

'Flynn!' She was truly shocked.

'The truth, please.'

'You...you're thirty-eight years old and used to full intimacy in your relationships.' She couldn't believe how priggish she sounded. Neither, apparently, could Flynn.

'Marigold, you haven't the faintest idea what I'm used to within a relationship,' he said coldly. 'Now, if this is your way of asking me if I've slept with women in the past then yes, I have. Hell, as you've just pointed out so baldly, I am a mature man, not some boy, wet behind the ears. However, I have never indulged in a promiscuous lifestyle, neither have I taken a woman to my bed who was not willing.'

She could certainly believe that. She stared at him miserably. No doubt they had been queueing up since Celine was crazy enough to let him go. 'The thing is...'

'Oh, not the thing again, please.'

The mocking note in his voice was the last straw, but it had the welcome advantage of putting iron in her backbone and fire in her eyes. All right, he wanted the truth, did he? He was darn well going to get it! 'I don't want to be someone who drifts in and out of your life,' she said tightly, 'that's all. That kind of lifestyle might suit some women just fine, but it wouldn't do for me. It might be old-fashioned but I would want to know that there at least is a chance of something permanent in the future if things worked out right. You...you're a closed and shut book.'

'I think the expression is an open and shut case.'

She glared at him. He knew exactly what she was getting at. She would not be a passing obsession, someone he wanted for a short time until the next challenge caught his fancy. And that was all she was, a challenge. If she'd gone to bed with him when he'd first wanted her to she might well be out of his life by now. And she couldn't cope with it. She loved him, and if she let him into her body as well as her heart she would never survive him leaving her.

It was when she'd met Flynn that she'd understood Dean had been all wrong for her, even if she hadn't admitted it for ages. From that first day Dean had ceased to matter. It was as simple, and as frightening, as that. She suddenly had the overwhelming desire to wail her head off, but controlled it rigidly.

'Marigold, correct me if I'm wrong, but wasn't it you

who insisted we keep each other at arm's length? Friends and no more? Don't tell me I'm now getting flak because I concurred with your desires?'

The word shivered over her and, although she was sure she hadn't betrayed herself, she was aware of the silvery eyes honing in on her. 'Come here,' he said softly.

'No, I need to make you understand we can't carry on like this. We live different lives; *we're* different. There's no meeting point. It's better to finish now…'

He moved, reaching her in a couple of strides and pulling her up from the sofa and into his arms. It was no gentle kiss; there was a well of frustration and pent-up passion that he hadn't let her see before, and Marigold was instantly aroused in spite of herself.

She found herself clutching him closer, accepting his kiss with a hunger which matched Flynn's, her mouth greedy for his. In seconds they were utterly lost to anything but each other, Marigold's arms tight round his shoulders as Flynn arched her backwards, his lips burning her throat before they moved back to take her mouth.

Somehow Marigold found that her coat was on the floor and then Flynn was nuzzling at the soft swell of her breasts above her low-cut lacy bra, her blouse open, although she had no recollection of Flynn undoing the tiny square pearl buttons. She was aware of the harsher material of his overcoat against her as he continued to ravish her flesh, the scent of him, the overall power and bigness of him, but only on the perimeter of her mind. The feverish need which had taken hold of her within seconds of his mouth taking hers had blurred everything but the desire to get closer and closer.

The soft pads of his fingertips had found her taut nipples under their flimsy covering and he was rubbing them gently, causing her to moan in her throat at the pleasure the small action produced. His body was imprinted against hers, his hard thighs and strong legs feeding the heady rush of sensation which had taken her over. She could feel his heart slamming against his ribcage and the tiny tremors shivering beneath her hands on his muscled shoulders, and knew he wanted her every bit as much as she wanted him.

He crushed her closer to him, lifting her right off her feet as he sank down on the sofa with her in his arms, settling her on his lap, his mouth never leaving hers. 'So soft, so warm, so perfect...' His voice was a thick, low murmur against her lips and she revelled in her power over this alien individual who had exploded into her life. 'You're sending me crazy, do you know that?'

For her answer she pressed herself against the solid wall of his chest, seeking his mouth with an urgency that was mindless.

'I want you, Marigold, but not like this. I want us to be able to take our time, can you understand that? I want to possess you so completely there'll be no room for anything but me in your head and your body. I want to marry you...'

The words hung on the air, shivering like tiny, crystallised raindrops caught in the delicate strands of a spider's web.

'What?' She drew back a little, staring at him dazedly. 'What did you say?'

'I want you to be my wife.' His hard looks had softened into such tenderness her breath caught in her throat. 'I agree with you, we can't carry on like this, not without me losing my sanity,' he added ruefully. 'You say we lead different lives so let's remedy that and lead one life together. You can still have your work, you can have the cottage as your studio if you like, somewhere where you can work peacefully and without interruption when I'm in London. When I'm home we can spend as much time together as we can.'

He had got it all worked out, she thought wonderingly. He must have been thinking about this for some time. 'But…but you never said anything before,' she murmured weakly.

'You made it clear I had to try the softly, softly approach,' Flynn said drily, 'and I can understand that after what you've been through. But you were right in one thing, Marigold—I am thirty-eight years old and frankly my time of stealing the odd kiss behind the bike sheds is long since past. I would have taken you to bed within days of us meeting if you had been willing, I admit it, but you weren't ready—in here.' He touched her forehead lightly with the tip of a finger.

'Flynn…' Her voice trailed away as she looked into his eyes, which were lit from within by a light which had turned them the hue of mother-of-pearl. 'Are…are you sure?'

'As you have so succinctly pointed out, I've been around long enough to know what I want and from whom,' Flynn said softly. 'But I never asked any of the others to marry me.'

Except Celine. The thought hammered in her mind for a second before she pushed it resolutely away. She couldn't begin to work this complex and highly intelligent individual out, but he was offering her more than she had ever dreamed he would. And she loved him. In fact she loved him so much she didn't know how she would have managed to live without him. And now she didn't have to.

'So what's your answer?' he said very quietly. 'Think

carefully before you speak but one thing is for sure; I'm not letting you go out of my life and my patience is exhausted. I need to make a statement to any other young whippersnappers like your ex that might be sniffing about, too—a statement that you are mine.'

A statement to other men? Was he mad? Did he really imagine she had them queueing up in droves? 'It doesn't look as if I've any other option than to say yes, then,' she said softly, her mouth tremulous. 'But I don't understand—'

He had cut her voice off with a long and passionate kiss, only lifting his mouth from hers when she was trembling against him, melting and soft. 'What don't you understand?'

'Why you want me,' she said with touching honesty.

He stroked the smooth silk of her cheek very gently. 'Then I'll have to make you understand,' he said huskily, his eyes telling her of his desire more eloquently than any words could have done. 'But now is not the time.'

He glanced at his watch. 'Hell, I've got to go. I only intended to call by briefly to explain something, but there's no time now. I've got to go. I'll ring you, OK? In the morning before you leave for work. It's important we talk.'

'Yes, all right.' She was bewildered, but he was already lifting her away from him and standing to his feet, clearly anxious to be off. 'Are you going to the hospital now?' she asked, already knowing the answer. She had noticed the expression which had come over his face before when he was heavily involved in a case—a kind of veiled urgency, as though part of him was already in the operating theatre.

'Uh-huh.' He kissed her again, long and hard. 'But I'll ring you in the morning,' he reiterated.

That meant he was probably going to be in Theatre until the early hours; the case must be a serious one that couldn't wait. No doubt even now the patient was going through the rigorous checks and procedures Flynn insisted on before he operated.

'You go,' Marigold said quickly, wanting to make it easy for him, and then, for the first time since they'd met, it was she who reached up on her tiptoes and kissed him.

Flynn swept her close again for one last scorching embrace before he left, buttoning his coat as he went.

For a full minute after Flynn had gone Marigold just leant against the front door, staring dazedly about her tiny hall. Of all the events of the day, Flynn's proposal of marriage was the most amazing and she just couldn't take it in. She ran their conversation through in her mind as though she was listening to a recording to convince herself it had actually happened.

Marigold Moreau… She blinked, putting her hand to her wildly beating heart. He had asked her to become his *wife*.

She tottered through to the kitchen and made herself a strong cup of coffee before taking it through to the sitting room. She couldn't eat anything, not yet, she was too excited and worked up. Oh, Flynn, Flynn… The enormity of it began to sink in. *Marriage*. It had all seemed so simple when he was here and holding her tight, but now she found herself wondering why he had asked her to marry him this particular night. Had she forced him into the proposal by the stance she had taken tonight and the way she'd been over the last months? Refusing to sleep with him? If so, she didn't want it to be like that. That would be like a form of sexual blackmail and never, not for a second, had she planned that.

In fact it had never crossed her mind that Flynn would ever ask her to become his wife; there was Celine Jenet, after all.

Marigold brushed her hair away from her hot face, shutting her eyes tightly for a moment or two as she struggled with her turbulent thoughts, and the more she struggled the more the old doubts and fears raised their heads.

Had Flynn said he loved her? She thought back to the emotion-charged minutes they had shared, her racing mind desperately seeking reassurance. No, he had not. Not in so many words. But the way he'd looked at her had been a declaration in itself, hadn't it?

Or—a little voice in the back of her mind asked probingly—was it that she wanted, *needed* to believe it had been a declaration?

Her head was whirling after a few minutes, and another cup of coffee—black this time and as strong as she could stand it—did nothing to clear her head.

She needed to switch off for a few minutes. Marigold reached for the TV remote, and as the little screen in front of her lit up she sank back against the soft cushions of the sofa, utterly spent.

She couldn't remember a thing about the programme which was on—she must have sat in a kind of stupor through most of it—but her attention was caught by the short clip introducing the next feature, an awards ceremony of some kind. 'Tonight promises to be a glittering occasion for those in the fashion world...' It went on in the same vein for a moment or two, but then Marigold sat up straight as the announcer said, 'And among those flying in this afternoon was Celine Jenet, who has only recently announced her retirement from the catwalk.' There was the briefest of pictures of a smiling Celine exiting the airport terminal, but it was the tall, dark man who had his arm round her waist who caught Marigold's eye.

Flynn. Marigold's hands went to cover her mouth, and she pressed hard against her flesh as she stared uncomprehendingly at the screen before the picture changed, showing more celebrities and flashing cameras and crowds cheering outside some building or other.

This afternoon. That was what the announcer had said. Celine was here, in London. With Flynn.

'No. Oh, no.' It was a whimper and Marigold heard herself with a feeling of self-disgust, but she could do nothing about the pain and shock swamping her.

Was that where Flynn was tonight? With Celine at this gala occasion? She clicked off the TV, her head swimming. And she had actually encouraged him to leave her, thinking he was going to the hospital.

A tide of nausea rose up in Marigold's throat and she found herself having to take deep breaths to control the sickness. How could he do this to her? Lie to her like this? How could he *propose* and then go straight to another woman, to Celine? He was as bad as Dean. A sob caught in her throat and she stood up, beginning to walk backwards and forwards as she tried to think what to do. History had repeated itself, it would seem. Was there something the matter with her? she asked herself wretchedly. There had to be. Something had to make these men think that she was stupid.

But…but what if by some hundred-to-one chance she had got it wrong? Maybe, just maybe he had met Celine at the airport for old times' sake? It was possible.

She knew she was clutching at straws but she couldn't help it. What if Flynn had been telling the truth and was at the hospital tonight? It didn't have to follow that because he had been with Celine that afternoon he was with her at this function tonight. But how could she find out for sure?

Bertha might know. Marigold's heart began to thump hard and she didn't wait to consider further, reaching for the telephone and dialling the Shropshire number which was written in the little book at the side of it. It was only as the receiver was picked up at the other end she realised she could have called the hospital; Bertha might have been told to deny he was with Celine.

Marigold thought quickly, and then said, 'Bertha? It's Marigold. I was calling to speak to Flynn but I've just remembered, he's with Celine, isn't he? I'd forgotten. It's been a hectic day with one thing and another and I'm not thinking straight.'

'That's all right, dear.'

She hadn't denied it. *She hadn't denied it.* 'I'll call him on his mobile later,' Marigold said hurriedly before Bertha could start chatting. 'I'm in a mad rush. Goodbye for now.'

She put down the phone without waiting for Bertha's reply and then sat staring at the receiver blankly. She hated him. She really, really hated him.

She looked up the number of his London flat and di-alled slowly. It was the answer machine on the other end of the line but she had expected that. She spoke clearly and concisely when the bleeps stopped. 'Flynn? It's Marigold. I hope you had a nice evening, you and Celine. Oh, just one more thing. I wouldn't marry you if you were the last man on earth. OK? And for the record I never did trust you, so don't think you fooled me for a minute. I don't want to hear from you or see you again. Goodbye.'

She put down the phone, blew a strand of hair out of her eyes and burst into tears.

CHAPTER NINE

MARIGOLD didn't know at what point she eventually fell asleep, but she had cried herself dry by the time she fell into bed at gone midnight and was exhausted in mind, body and spirit. Nevertheless, she tossed and turned for what seemed like hours before drifting off into a troubled slumber.

When the telephone began to jar her back to consciousness it took some time for the insistent tone to register. She finally surfaced, pulling herself up in bed and reaching for the receiver as she tried to focus blurry eyes on her alarm clock. Five o'clock in the morning?

And then, as a furious male voice bit out her name, it all came flooding back and she remembered. Flynn and Celine!

'What the hell is that message supposed to mean?' Flynn sounded more angry than she had ever heard him.

Marigold desperately tried to gather thoughts that were still buried in layers of cotton wool. 'I would have thought it was pretty obvious,' she managed fairly smartly, considering her heart had just jumped up into her throat at the sound of his voice.

'You know about Celine?'

Marigold blinked, unable to believe her ears for a moment. He wasn't even going to *try* to deny it? Perversely that made her madder than ever. 'Again, I would have thought that was obvious,' she said icily.

'Then what was with the crack about a nice evening?' he snarled savagely. 'And me fooling you?'

She had never heard him like this, not even when he had thought she was Emma. He obviously didn't take kindly to being caught out. 'I said you *didn't* fool me,' she reminded him cuttingly.

'You also said you didn't want to see or hear from me again a few hours after promising to become my wife,' he grated, 'so what the hell is this about? And don't say you think it's obvious because it damn well isn't, not to me. I've been up for twenty-four hours and I'm not in the mood to play games, Marigold.'

Games! He thought this was a game, did he? And he had obviously only just got in. 'You told me you were at the hospital last night,' Marigold said, refusing to let her voice quiver.

'So?'

'So I saw a clip on TV of Celine arriving in London,' Marigold said tightly. 'You were with her. And Bertha said you were with her last night.' Well, she had in a way.

'Wait a minute, let's get this straight. You said you knew about Celine?'

'I do. There was a programme about the fashion awards, all very glitzy and glamorous,' Marigold said scathingly.

'And you think Celine was there last night?' There was the briefest of pauses. And then his voice had changed to a soft, icy tone when he said, 'And you phoned Bertha to see if I was with Celine at this do? Is that right?'

'Yes.' There was something wrong here. Her stomach curdled with horrible premonition.

'You could have called me on my mobile, or phoned the hospital if you wanted to talk to me direct, Marigold.'

'You…you weren't at the hospital.'

'Did you check? Before you talked to Bertha?' he asked, still in the quiet, deadly tone which was sending chills of foreboding all over her body.

'No.'

'I wasn't worth one phone call.'

'It wasn't like that,' she protested faintly.

'The hell it wasn't.'

'I thought—'

'I know what you thought, Marigold. You were sure I was fooling around with Celine last night so you called Bertha to check up on me. Damn it, I've been such a fool. I thought I could make you love me the way I love you, but you never gave me a chance, not really, did you? Apart from the physical attraction between us I don't think you even like me.'

'Flynn, that's not true.'

Her genuine distress didn't impress him at all. 'You believed I would ask you to marry me and then go out and spend the night with another woman.'

The contempt in his voice cut Marigold to the quick, the more so because it was the truth. What could she say, what could she do to make this right? Whatever had occurred during the day she believed Flynn had been at the hospital last night. He hadn't been with Celine.

And then he proved her wrong when he said bitterly, 'I *was* with Celine last night, Marigold. I left her at four this morning. She's in Intensive Care after having a tumour the size of a golf ball removed from her head. When she comes round—*if* she comes round—she'll probably have to learn to walk and talk again; she might be blind or worse. She should have been operated on weeks ago but some charlatan of a doctor she visited missed all the signs of a tumour and told her she was having migraines due to stress.'

Marigold was frozen with horror.

'She came to see me yesterday for a second opinion; she was never intending to go to any function. I knew I had to operate immediately from the tests I did in the afternoon but until we opened up the skull no one realised how bad it was.'

'Flynn, I'm so sorry.' Remorse and shame were strangling her voice. 'I don't know what to say.'

'There's nothing left to say.' It was terribly final. 'I was fooling myself all along there was anything real between us.'

'No, please! Listen to me. I didn't understand—'

'No, you didn't, but then I wasn't important enough to you for you to make the effort, was I?' he said bitterly. 'If you thought I was capable of behaving like that then there is no hope. I've tried to show you myself over the last months, Marigold. The inner man if you like.' It was said with cutting self-derision. 'I've never pretended to be perfect, but neither am I the slimeball you've got me down for.'

'I haven't. Flynn, I haven't.' She was crying now but it seemed to have no effect on him at all.

'You are going to have to trust someone some time, Marigold,' he said flatly, 'but it won't be me.'

He meant it, she thought sickly. She'd lost him.

'Goodbye, Marigold.' And the phone was put down very quietly.

The next few days were the worst of Marigold's life. She got through the working hours by functioning on automatic pilot, but once she was home, in the endless loneliness of her little flat, there was no opiate to the pain of bitter self-reproach and guilt.

She picked up the telephone to call Flynn a hundred times a night, but always put it down again without making the call. What could she say after all? She'd let him down in the worst manner possible and there was no way back. She hadn't even given him the opportunity to defend himself before she had sailed in, all guns firing. He must have got home from the hospital, exhausted and mentally and emotionally drained, and then had the welcome of her telephone message.

If she said she loved him now he would never believe her—she certainly hadn't acted like a woman in love, she flailed herself wretchedly. Love believed the best of the beloved; it was generous and understanding and tender.

She deserved his hatred and contempt. She deserved all the pain and regret.

This orgy of self-recrimination continued until the weekend, and then two things happened which jolted Marigold out of her hopelessness, the first event instigating the second.

At half-past nine in the morning on a cold but bright Saturday Marigold answered a knock at the door to find Dean on her doorstep, an enormous bunch of flowers in his hand. He spoke quickly before she could say a word. 'I've come to ask if we can still be friends, just friends,' he said quietly, not sounding like himself at all. 'It was the truth when I said I missed you, Dee, and I don't want it to end like this. I know you're involved with someone else and I don't blame you, but I'd like to think we can still ring each other now and again, meet for coffee, things like that. What do you think?'

She stared at him in astonishment, seeing the genuine

desire for reconciliation, and then surprised them both by bursting into tears.

Two cups of coffee and a couple of rounds of toast later Marigold found herself in the extraordinary position of—having cried on Dean's shoulder—being encouraged by her ex-fiancé to chase after another man. 'If I thought there was the inkling of a chance of us getting back together I wouldn't be saying this,' Dean admitted wryly, 'but there isn't, is there?'

Marigold shook her head, her mouth being full of toast and Marmite.

'And I feel a bit responsible you didn't trust Flynn as you would have done if I hadn't played fast and loose,' Dean said in such a way Marigold suspected he expected her to deny he was to blame.

'Good, you should,' she responded firmly after swallowing the toast.

'Yeah, right.' He drained his coffee-cup, aware the time of Marigold seeing him through rose-coloured spectacles was well and truly over. 'So, go and see him. Talk to him face to face. Tell it how it is. Grovel if you have to. If you don't you'll spend the rest of your life wondering if things might have been OK if you'd just tried.'

Marigold stared at him. Comfort came in the oddest ways and from sources you least expected.

Once Dean had left she ran herself a hot bath and lay soaking in strawberry bubbles as she considered all they had said. If someone like Dean, essentially pretty shallow and selfish, could make the grand gesture he had made this morning, it surely wasn't beyond her to do something similar for Flynn, was it? OK, so Flynn might cut her dead or reduce her to nothing with that cynical tongue of his, but what did that matter? If that happened she deserved it, and she had no pride left after the misery of the last few days. She would do anything, *anything* to show him how sorry she was.

He had said he loved her, in that last terrible phone call, and she believed he had. Perhaps he still did? Perhaps she hadn't destroyed everything? And even if Celine *was* his first love she didn't care any more. It was *her* he had proposed to a few nights ago, *their* future he had been thinking about.

Marigold had rung the hospital a few times, enquiring after Celine, but each time she had got a standard formal reply. 'Miss Jenet is as well as can be expected.' The last two days she hadn't rung at all, but once out of the bath she picked up the phone and dialled the number of Flynn's home in Shropshire.

'Bertha?' She took a deep breath after hearing Flynn's housekeeper's voice. 'It's Marigold. I'm ringing to ask how Celine is.'

'Oh, hello, dear.' From the tone of Bertha's voice she knew nothing about their break-up, and this seemed to be borne out when Bertha said, her voice a little puzzled, 'Why don't you ask Mr Moreau, dear?'

'He's so busy.'

'Oh, you don't have to tell me! He'll be ill if he carries on, but hopefully now Celine is on the mend he can relax a bit more. She's still progressing little by little, dear, but she was awake more yesterday and her speech is all but back. It's a blessing her eyesight hasn't been affected, isn't it? I think that's what was worrying Mr Moreau the most.'

By the time Marigold put down the phone a few minutes later she was trembling with reaction. Celine was all right; she was going to get better. According to Bertha, Flynn was confident he had removed all of the tumour and the prognosis for the future was good.

She was going to go round to his flat as soon as she was dressed. She had to see him now, today. She needed to make him understand she loved him, really loved him, and then the rest was up to him. If he couldn't forgive her... She dared not let herself think about that. If she did she would revert to the soggy mess of the last few days, and right now she had to be strong.

After blow-drying her hair into a shining, sleek shoulder-length style, she stood for some time surveying the contents of her wardrobe. She needed to look smart but not too smart; feminine and appealing but not too obvious.

Eventually she chose a pair of new smart brown trousers with her brown boots, teaming them with a white cashmere jumper which had been wickedly expensive but always made her feel good. She made up her face with just a smidgen of foundation to hide the paleness of nerves, and stroked a couple of coats of mascara on her eyelashes.

She couldn't compete with Celine in the beauty stakes, she thought soberly, and she wasn't going to try. This was her; five feet four, brown hair, blue eyes, and capable of the utmost stupidity as her behaviour a few days ago had proved. Would he talk to her? She shut her eyes tightly and prayed for strength. She'd make him!

As the taxi pulled into the beautifully kept grounds of the private hospital Marigold did a few deep-breathing exercises to try and combat her wildly beating heart.

She had gone to Flynn's London flat first but when there had been no answer had assumed he was at the hospital. Of course, he might not be, she reminded herself nervously, but he was bound to turn up here sooner or later. Considering the taxi had run up a bill equal to a small mortgage, she wasn't budging further anyway!

After paying the taxi driver, she squared her shoulders under her brown leather jacket and marched purposefully to the reception doors, which glided open at her approach. She waded through ankle-deep carpet to where an exquisitely coiffured receptionist was waiting with a charming smile. 'Can I help you?' she purred sweetly.

'I would like to speak to Mr Moreau. Mr Flynn Moreau,' Marigold said firmly.

'Do you have an appointment?'

'No, I don't have an appointment.'

'Then I'm really very sorry but—'

'I'm not a patient of Mr Moreau's,' Marigold said quickly. 'I'm a friend. I'm sure he will want to see me when he knows I'm here.' She was getting better at lying, Marigold thought a trifle hysterically. That one had come out as smooth as cream.

A couple of men walked down some stairs at the far end of the reception area, obviously from the Middle East as their flowing robes proclaimed. They looked as though they owned a couple of countries apiece at least.

'Mr Moreau's secretary is not in today but I'll see if I can contact him,' the receptionist said pleasantly. 'I'm really not sure if he is in the building.'

Oh, yes, right, Marigold thought disbelievingly. If Flynn thought she was a poor liar he ought to listen to this woman!

'Who shall I say wants him?'

'Miss Flower.' She was not going to give her first name to this vision of sophistication!

'If you would like to take a seat, Miss Flower , I'll see what I can do.' The receptionist waved a pale be-ringed hand with long, perfectly painted red talons in the direction of several pale cream sofas some distance away, and Marigold had no choice but to smile politely and comply.

She could see the woman talking on a telephone from where she was seated but was too far away to hear what she was saying, although once or twice the heavily made-up, almond-shaped eyes looked her way. As the receptionist replaced one telephone another rang at the side of her, and she was once again engrossed in conversation.

The Middle Eastern gentlemen had been standing talking in low voices, and as they now departed in a swish of long robes and exclusive perfume Marigold glanced about her, trying not to appear overawed. Money might not be able to buy good health but it certainly made being sick more enjoyable! She knew Flynn worked in the public sector at the local hospital as well as this private one, and the two places must be like two different worlds. Suddenly panic was making her throat dry. She should never have come. This was a big mistake. Celine was far more suited to his world than she was and now the other woman was ill Flynn might well be hoping they would get back together again.

'Hello, Marigold.'

For the first time in her life she knew what it was to have her heart stop dead as the quiet, deep voice sounded just behind her left shoulder. She swung round so quickly she nearly fell off the sofa, and then jumped to her feet in a totally uncool way. 'Flynn! I...I didn't hear you.'

He raked back an errant lock of hair from his forehead, a slow gesture which suggested his air of calmness was deliberate. 'Sophia said you were here asking for me.'

He looked terrible. As handsome as ever and so sexy he should be certified as dangerous, but there was a grey tinge to the tanned skin that spoke of extreme exhaustion and his mouth wasn't just stern but drawn and tight. A sudden thought crossed her mind and she said quickly, 'Celine? She *is* all right. Bertha said she was getting better.'

'Celine is fine.'

He was wearing a pale blue shirt and his hands were thrust in the pockets of his suit trousers, his tie hanging askew as it so often did. She felt such a flood of love rise up in her that she wanted to cry. Instead she said shakily, 'I'm sorry to bother you here but I had to talk to you. The…receptionist said she didn't know if you were here or not.'

He shrugged powerful shoulders. 'It's been a hectic few days. There was a bad pile-up on the motorway and I've been to-ing and fro-ing between hospitals.'

She nodded. So that was why he looked dead beat. For a moment, a crazy moment she had just wondered if it was because he had been thinking about her.

His eyes narrowed slightly as they focused on the silky veil of her hair for a moment before taking in her smart trousers and the figure-hugging cashmere sweater. 'You're obviously on your way out to lunch somewhere,' he said dismissively. 'How can I help you?'

For a second she almost turned tail and ran in the face of his cool indifference, but something in the way he was standing, the faintest indication that his hands were balled fists in his pockets, caused her to stand her ground. 'I'm not going out to lunch,' she said evenly, her voice not shaking any more. 'I came to see you.'

'Why?'

It was now or never. 'To tell you I love you,' she said very clearly.

'Go home, Marigold.'

But she had seen his eyes flicker and the grimace of pain—fleeting but definitely there—that had twisted his mouth as she had spoken.

'Not until I am sure you understand how I feel,' she said thickly. 'If you walk away now I shall follow you. I'm not afraid to cause a scene.'

She saw his eyes widen just for a moment and then he took her arm, his voice grim as he said, 'This is ridiculous but if you insist you had better come to my office. This is a hospital, in case you'd forgotten.'

His office was sumptuous with a view over bowling-green-smooth lawns and mature trees, but Marigold didn't notice the decor. Once Flynn had shut the door he walked over to his desk, perching on the edge of it as he waved her to one of the visitor's chairs in front of it. 'I'm due in a meeting shortly so I can only spare you five minutes.' It was the cool, calm voice of a stranger, unemotional, cold.

She ignored the seat and walked across to stand right in front of him, so close she could see the five o'clock shadow on his chin although it was only midday. She touched his face lightly and though he didn't move a muscle she knew he had tensed. 'You need a new blade in your razor,' she said softly.

Her words were followed by a silence which slowly began to vibrate, an electricity in the air that was almost tangible. He remained perfectly still as he said, 'I've been up since two in the morning; complications with one of the road-accident victims. I've got an electric razor in my desk; I'll use that later.'

She put her arms round his neck. 'Flynn,' she said

quietly, 'please forgive me. I love you with all my heart. Please marry me.'

She could feel him begin to tremble but his voice was perfectly under control when he said, 'You don't have to do this, Marigold. I'm a big boy, I can survive rejection.' He reached up to remove her arms from round his neck but she hung on tight, nearly throttling him.

'Listen to me,' she said fiercely, her heart suddenly blazing with hope because she knew, she *knew* he still loved her. 'I love you, I do. I loved you almost from the beginning but I didn't dare admit it to myself. It was too soon after Dean for one thing but that wasn't really it. I knew you had the potential to hurt me in a way Dean never could have done, that was the thing.'

'The thing again.' He was trying to be mocking but it didn't come off and they both knew it.

'And then I heard those women talking about this girl that you still loved, this beauty who was always there in the background. It was my worst fear come true. And she turned out to be not just some ordinary woman but Celine Jenet, one of the most beautiful women in the world. I could understand how no one could compare with her. I thought you were waiting until she wanted you again.'

'Wanted me again?' His hands weren't trying to untangle hers now but holding them against his neck. 'Marigold, it was me who broke off the engagement, not Celine. I realised I loved her like a sister, a best friend, and after a time she came to realise that that wouldn't have been enough. If we'd married we would have made each other very unhappy.'

Why hadn't she considered it might have been Flynn who finished it? *Because she loved him too much.*

'I was jealous,' she whispered, her eyes shining with

tears. 'And I didn't trust you. I don't deserve another chance...'

He slid off the desk, pulling her into him and kissing her until she was drowning in bliss. 'I love you, Marigold Flower,' he murmured huskily. 'I'll always love you. I loved you when I thought you didn't love or want me, and it was slowly crucifying me. I've never felt this way before. I have lived for thirty-eight years without knowing what real love was, until I met you. Do you believe that?'

'Yes, yes, I do.' Her eyes were shining and his mouth sought hers again, his hands moving over her body, touching her with sensual, intimate caresses.

'You're everything I've ever wanted, although I couldn't have said what I was looking for until I saw you. Then it all came together in a moment of time, and I knew. Does that make sense, sweetheart?'

'I don't know.' Marigold didn't know anything when she was close to him like this, except that she never wanted to be anywhere else in the whole of her life.

'And you fought me every inch of the way.' He took her mouth again in a long, hungry kiss. 'I was the enemy, and whatever I did, however I tried to show you that we belonged together, you wouldn't give in.'

He made her sound almost brave, Marigold thought ruefully, when really she had been muddled and confused and frightened to death half the time, frightened of her feelings and the desire she'd felt every time he touched her.

'Ask me again.'

'What?'

He had pulled away slightly to look into her radiant face, and now his voice was soft and husky when he said, 'Ask me to marry you again. And before you do I want you to know that it will be forever. Once I say yes, there's no going back, Marigold Flower. Whatever happens you're mine.'

'Flynn Moreau, will you marry me?' she asked gently, cradling his face in her hands as she let him see all the love in her heart. 'Will you be my husband and the father of my babies? Will you grow old with me and watch our grandchildren play through mellow summer days, and will you still be my love?'

'Yes,' he said, his voice gruff.

And she kissed him.

Favorite Harlequin Intrigue® author

REBECCA YORK

brings you a special 3-in-1 volume featuring her famous 43 Light Street miniseries.

Dark Secrets

"Rebecca York's 43 Light Street series just keeps getting better and better!"
—*Romantic Times*

Available in December 2002 wherever paperbacks are sold.

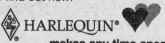

International
bestselling author

Miranda
LEE

Brings you the final three
novels in her famous
Hearts of Fire miniseries...

FORTUNE & FATE

The passion, scandal and
hopes of Australia's
fabulously wealthy
Whitmore family promise
riveting reading in this
special volume containing
three full-length novels.

*Available in January 2003 at
your favorite retail outlet.*

HARLEQUIN®
Makes any time special ®

Harlequin is proud to have published
more than 75 novels by

Emma Darcy

Award-
winning Australian
author **Emma Darcy** is a
unique voice in Harlequin
Presents®. Her compelling, sexy,
intensely emotional novels have
gripped the imagination of readers
around the globe, and she's sold
nearly 60 million books
worldwide.

Praise for Emma Darcy:

"Emma Darcy delivers a spicy love story…a fiery conflict
and a hot sensuality."

"Emma Darcy creates a strong emotional premise
and a sizzling sensuality."

"Emma Darcy pulls no punches."

"With exciting scenes, vibrant characters and a layered story line,
Emma Darcy dishes up a spicy reading experience."

—*Romantic Times Magazine*

**Look out for more thrilling stories by Emma Darcy,
coming soon in**

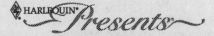

INTEMMA